CRUCIAL INSTANCES

BY EDITH WHARTON
AUTHOR OF "A GIFT FROM THE GRAVE"

LONDON
JOHN MURRAY, ALBEMARLE STREET 1901

Edith Wharton (born Edith Newbold Jones; January 24, 1862 – August 11, 1937) was an American novelist, short story writer, and designer. Wharton combined an insider's view of American aristocracy with a powerful prose style. Her novels and short stories realistically portrayed the lives and morals of the late nineteenth century, an era of decline and faded wealth. She won the Pulitzer Prize for Literature in 1921, and was the first woman to receive this honor. Wharton was acquainted with many of the well-known people of her day, both in America and in Europe, including President Theodore Roosevelt.

Edith Wharton was born Edith Newbold Jones to George Frederic Jones and Lucretia Stevens Rhinelander at their brownstone at 14 West Twenty-third Street in New York City. She had two older brothers, Frederic Rhinelander, who was sixteen, and Henry Edward, who was eleven. She was baptized April 20, 1862, Easter Sunday, at Grace Church. To her friends and family she was known as "Pussy Jones." The saying "keeping up with the Joneses" is said to refer to her father's family. She was also related to the Rensselaers, the most prestigious of the old patroon families, who had received land grants from the former Dutch government of New York and New Jersey. She had a lifelong friendship with her niece, the landscape architect Beatrix Farrand of Reef Point in Bar Harbor, Maine.

Wharton was born during the Civil War; she was three years old when the Confederate States surrendered. After the war, the family traveled extensively in Europe. From 1866 to 1872, the Jones family visited France, Italy, Germany, and Spain. During her travels, the young Edith became fluent in French, German, and Italian. At the age of ten, she suffered from typhoid fever while the family was at a spa in the Black Forest. After the family returned to the United States in 1872, they spent their winters in New York and their summers in Newport, Rhode Island.While in Europe, she was educated by tutors and governesses. She rejected the standards of fashion and etiquette that were expected of young girls at the time, which were intended to allow women to marry well and to be put on display at balls and parties. She considered these fashions superficial and oppressive. Edith wanted more education than she received, so she read from her father's library and from the libraries of her father's friends. Her mother forbade her to read novels until she was married, and Edith obeyed this command.Wharton began writing poetry and fiction as a young girl, and attempted to write her first novel at age eleven. At age 15, her first published work appeared, a translation of a German poem "Was die Steine Erzählen" ("What the Stones Tell") by Heinrich Karl Brugsch, for which which she was paid $50. Her family did not want her name to appear in print, since writing was not considered a proper occupation for a society woman of her time. Consequently, the poem was published under the name of a friend's father, E. A. Washburn, a cousin of Ralph Waldo Emerson who supported women's education. He played a pivotal role in Edith's efforts to educate herself and encouraged her ambition to write professionally. In 1877, at the age of 15, she secretly wrote a 30,000 word novella "Fast and Loose." In 1878 her father arranged for a collection of two dozen original poems and five translations, Verses, to be privately published. In 1880 she had five poems published anonymously in the Atlantic Monthly, an important literary magazine. Despite these early successes, she was not encouraged by her family or her social circle, and though she continued to write, she did not publish anything more until her poem "The Last Giustiniani" was published in Scribner's Magazine in October 1889.On 29 April 1885, at age 23, she married Edward (Teddy) Robbins Wharton, who was 12 years her senior, at the Trinity Chapel Complex.From a well-established Boston family, he was a sportsman and a gentleman of the same social class and shared her love of travel. From the late 1880s until 1902, he suffered acute depression, and the couple ceased their extensive travel. At that time his depression manifested as a more serious disorder, after which they lived almost exclusively at their estate The Mount. In 1908 her husband's mental state was determined to be incurable. In the same year, she began an affair with Morton Fullerton, a journalist for The Times, in whom she found an intellectual partner. She divorced Edward Wharton in 1913 after 28 years of marriage. Around the same time, Edith was beset with harsh criticisms leveled by the naturalist writers.

In addition to novels, Wharton wrote at least 85 short stories. She was also a garden designer, interior designer, and a taste-maker of her time. She wrote several design books, including her first major published work, The Decoration of Houses (1897), co-authored by Ogden Codman. Another of her "home and garden" books is the generously illustrated Italian Villas and Their Gardens of 1904.

CONTENTS

I
THE DUCHESS AT PRAYER 1

II
THE ANGEL AT THE GRAVE 45

III
THE RECOVERY 83

IV
"COPY": A DIALOGUE 125

V
THE REMBRANDT 155

VI
THE MOVING FINGER 191

VII
THE CONFESSIONAL 227

THE DUCHESS AT PRAYER

THE DUCHESS AT PRAYER
HAVE you ever questioned the long shuttered front of an old Italian house, that motionless mask, smooth, mute, equivocal as the face of a priest behind which buzz the secrets of the confessional? Other houses declare the activities they shelter; they are the clear expressive cuticle of a life flowing close to the surface; but the old palace in its narrow street, the villa on its cypress-hooded hill, are as impenetrable as death. The tall windows are like blind eyes, the great door is a shut mouth. Inside there may be sunshine, the scent of myrtles, and a pulse of life through all the arteries of the huge frame; or a mortal solitude, where bats lodge in the disjointed stones and the keys rust in unused doors. . . .

fold on fold of the oldest man I had back into the post that: Eke a memory than a wnn toe artnal was toe Irsjly witn wlnai

"Since I can remember."

I looked into his eyes; they were like tarnished metal mirrors reflecting nothing. "That must be a long time," I said involuntarily.

"A long time," he assented.

I looked down on the gardens. An opulence of dahlias overran the box-borders, between cypresses that cut the sunshine like basalt shafts. Bees hung above the lavender; lizards sunned themselves on the benches and slipped through the cracks of the dry basins. Everywhere were vanishing traces of that fantastic horticulture of which our dull age has lost the art. Down the alleys maimed statues stretched their arms like rows of whining beggars; faun-eared terms grinned in the thickets, and above the laurustinus walls rose the mock ruin of a temple, falling into real ruin in the bright disintegrating air. The glare was blinding.

"Let us go in," I said.

The old man pushed open a heavy door, behind which the cold lurked like a knife.

"The Duchess's apartments," he said.

Overhead and around us the same evanescent frescoes, under foot the same scagliola volutes, unrolled themselves interminably. Ebony cabinets, with inlay of precious marbles in cunning perspective, alternated down the room with the tarnished efflorescence of gilt consoles supporting Chinese monsters; and from the chimney-panel a gentleman in the Spanish habit haughtily ignored us.

"Duke Ercole II.," the old man explained, "by the Genoese Priest."

It was a narrow-browed face, sallow as a wax effigy, high-nosed and cautious-lidded, as though modelled by priestly hands; the lips weak and vain rather than cruel; a quibbling mouth that would have snapped at verbal errors like a lizard catching flies, but had never learned the shape of a round yes or no. One of the Duke's hands rested on the head of a dwarf, a simian creature with pearl earrings and fantastic dress; the other turned the pages of a folio propped on a skull.

"Beyond is the Duchess's bedroom," the old man reminded me.

Here the shutters admitted but two narrow shafts of light, gold bars deepening the subaqueous gloom. On a dais the bedstead, grim, nuptial, official, lifted its baldachin; a yellow Christ agonized between the curtains, and across the room a lady smiled at us from the chimney-breast.

The old man unbarred a shutter and the light touched her face. Such a face it was, with a flicker of laughter over it like the wind on a June meadow, and a singular tender pliancy of mien, as though one of Tiepolo's lenient goddesses had been busked into the stiff sheath of a seventeenth-century dress!

" No one has slept here," said the old man, " since the Duchess Violante."

" And she was ?"

" The lady there—first Duchess of Duke Ercole II."

He drew a key from his pocket and unlocked a door at the farther end of the room. " The chapel," he said. " This is the Duchess's balcony." As I turned to follow him the Duchess tossed me a sidelong smile.

1 stepped into a grated tribune above a chapel festooned with stucco. Pictures of bituminous saints mouldered between the pilasters; the artificial roses in the altar vases were grey with dust and age, and under the cobwebby rosettes of the vaulting a bird's nest clung. Before the altar stood a row of tattered arm-chairs, and I drew back at sight of a figure kneeling near them.

" The Duchess," the old man whispered. " By the Cavaliere Bernini."

It was the image of a woman in furred robes and spreading fraise, her hand lifted, her face addressed to the tabernacle. There was a strangeness in the sight of that immovable presence locked in prayer before an abandoned shrine. Her face was hidden, and I wondered whether it were grief or gratitude that raised her hands and drew her eyes to the altar, where no living prayer joined her marble invocation. I followed my guide down the tribune steps, impatient to see what mystic version of such terrestrial graces the ingenious artist had found —the Cavaliere was master of such arts. The Duchess's attitude was one of transport, as though heavenly airs fluttered her laces and the love-locks escaping from her coif. 1 saw how admirably the sculptor had caught the pose of her head, the tender slope of the shoulder; then I crossed over and looked into her face — it was a frozen horror. Never have hate, revolt, and agony so possessed a human countenance. . . .

The old man crossed himself and shuffled his feet on the marble.

" The Duchess Violante," he repeated.

" The same as in the picture ?"

" Eh—the same."

" But the face—what does it mean ? "

He shrugged his shoulders and turned deaf eyes on me. Then he shot a glance round the sepulchral place, clutched my sleeve and said, close to my ear: " It was not always so."

" What was not ?"

" The face—so terrible."

" The Duchess's face ?"

" The statue's. It changed after "

"After?"

" It was put here."

" The statue's face changed ? "

He mistook my bewilderment for incredulity, and his confidential finger dropped from my sleeve. "Eh, that's the story. I tell what I've heard. What do I know?" He resumed his senile shuffle across the marble. "This is a bad place to stay in—no one comes here.

It's too cold. But the gentleman said, *I must see everything!*"

I let the lire sound. "So I must—and hear everything. This story, now—from whom did you have it?"

His hand stole back. "One that saw it, by God!"

"That saw it?"

"My grandmother, then. I'm a very old man."

"Your grandmother? Your grandmother was?"

"The Duchess's serving girl, with respect to you."

"Your grandmother? Two hundred years ago?"

"Is it too long ago? That's as God pleases. I am a very old man, and she was a very old woman when I was born. When she died she was as black as a miraculous virgin, and her breath whistled like the wind in a keyhole. She told me the story when I was a little boy. She told it to me out there in the garden, on a bench by the fish pond, one summer night of the year she died. It must be true, for I can show you the very bench we sat on.

III

NOON lay heavier on the gardens; not our live humming warmth but the stale exhalation of dead summers. The very statues seemed to drowse like watches by a dead-bed. Lizards shot out of the cracked soil like flames, and the bench in the laurustinus niche was strewn with the blue varnished bodies of dead flies. Before us lay the fish pond, a yellow marble slab above rotting secrets. The villa looked across it, composed as a dead face, with the cypresses flanking it for candles.

IV

"IMPOSSIBLE, you say, that my mother's mother should have been the Duchess's maid? What do I know? It is so long since anything has happened here that the old things seem nearer, perhaps, than to those who live in cities. . . . But how else did she know about the statue then? Answer me that, sir! That she saw with her eyes, I can swear to, and never smiled again, so she told me, till they put her first child in her arms; . . . for she was taken to wife by the steward's son, Antonio, the same who had carried the letters. . . . But where am I? Ah, well . . . she was a mere slip, you understand, my grandmother, when the Duchess died, a niece of the upper maid, Nencia, and suffered about the Duchess because of her pranks and the funny songs she knew. It's possible, you think, she may have heard from others what she afterward fancied she had seen herself? How that is, it's not for an unlettered man to say; though indeed I myself seem to have seen many of the things she told me. This is a strange place. No one comes here, nothing changes, and the old memories stand up as distinct as the statues in the garden. . . .

"It began the summer after they came back from the Brenta. Duke Ercole had married the lady from Venice, you must know; it was a gay city, then, I'm told, with laughter and music on the water, and the days slipped by like boats running with the tide. Well, to humour her, he took her back the first autumn to the Brenta. Her father, it appears, had a grand palace there, with such gardens, bowling-alleys, grottoes, and casinos as never were; gondolas bobbing at the water-gates, a stable full of gilt coaches, a theatre full of players, and kitchens and offices full of cooks and lackeys to serve up chocolate all day long to the fine ladies in masks and furbelows, with their pet dogs and their blackamoors and their abates. Eh ! I know it all as if I'd been there; for Nencia, you see, my grandmother's aunt, travelled with the Duchess, and came back with her eyes round as platters, and not a word to say for the rest of the year to any of the lads who'd courted her here in Vicenza. "What happened there I don't know — my grandmother could never get at the rights of it, for Nencia was mute as a fish where her lady was concerned— but when they came back to Vicenza the Duke ordered the villa set in order; and in the spring he brought the Duchess here and left her. She looked happy enough, my grandmother said, and seemed no object for pity. Perhaps, after all, it was better than being shut up in Vicenza, in the tall painted rooms where priests came and went as softly as cats prowling for birds, and the Duke was for ever closeted in his library, talking with learned men. The Duke was a scholar; you noticed he was painted with a book? Well, those that can read 'em make out that they're full of wonderful things; as a man that's been to a fair across the mountains will always tell his people at home it was beyond anything they II ever see. As for the Duchess, she was all for music, play-acting, and young company. The Duke was a silent man, stepping quietly, with his eyes down, as though he'd just come from confession; when the Duchess's lap-dog yapped at his heels he danced like a man in a swarm of hornets; when the Duchess laughed he winced as if you'd drawn a diamond across a window-pane. And the Duchess was always laughing.

" When she first came to the villa she was very busy laying out the gardens, designing grottoes, planting groves and planning all manner of agreeable surprises in the way of water-jets that drenched you unexpectedly, and hermits in caves, and wild men that jumped at you out of thickets. She had a very pretty taste in such matters, but after a while she tired of it, and there being no one for her to talk to but her maids and the chaplain—a clumsy man deep in his books—why, she would have strolling players out from Vicenza, mountebanks and fortune-tellers from the marketplace, travelling doctors and astrologers, and all manner of trained animals. Still it could be seen that the poor lady pined for company, and her waiting women, who loved her, were glad when the Cavaliere Ascanio, the Duke's cousin, came to live at the vineyard across the valley—you see the pinkish house over there in the mulberries, with a red roof and a pigeon-cote ?

"The Cavaliere Ascanio was a cadet of one of the great Venetian houses, pezzi grossi of the Golden Book. He had been meant for the Church, I believe, but what! he set fighting above praying, and cast in his lot with the captain of the Duke of Mantua's brawi, himself a Venetian of good standing, but a little at odds with the law. Well, the next I know, the Cavaliere was in Venice again, perhaps not in good odour on account of his connection with the gentleman I speak of. Some say he tried to carry off a nun from the convent of Santa Croce; how that may be I can't say; but my grandmother declared he had enemies there, and the end of it was that on some pretext or other the Ten banished him to Vicenza. There, of course, the Duke, being his kinsman, had to show him a civil face; and that was how he first came to the villa.

" He was a fine young man, beautiful as a Saint Sebastian, a rare musician, who sang his own songs to the lute in a way that used to make my grandmother's heart melt and run through her body like mulled wine. He had a good word for everybody, too, and was always dressed in the French fashion, and smelt as sweet as a bean-field, and every soul about the place welcomed the sight of him.

"Well, the Duchess, it seemed, welcomed it too ; youth will have youth, and laughter turns to laughter; and the two matched each other like the candlesticks on an altar. The Duchess — you've seen her portrait—but to hear my grandmother, sir, it no more approached her than a weed comes up to a rose. The Cavaliere, indeed, as became a poet, paragoned her in his song to all the Pagan goddesses of antiquity; and doubtless these were finer to look at than mere women; but so, it seemed, was she; for, to believe my grandmother, she made other women look no more than the big French fashion-doll that used to be shown on Ascension days in the Piazza. She was one, at any rate, that needed no outlandish finery to beautify her; whatever dress she wore became her as feathers fit the bird; and her hair didn't get its colour by bleaching on the housetop. It glittered of itself like the threads in an Easter chasuble, and her skin was whiter than fine wheaten bread and her mouth as sweet as a ripe fig. . .

"Well, sir, you could no more keep them apart than the bees and the lavender. They were always together, singing, bowling, playing cup and ball, walking in the gardens, visiting the aviaries, and petting her Grace's trick-dogs and monkeys. The Duchess was as gay as a foal, always playing pranks and laughing, tricking out her animals like comedians, disguising herself as a peasant or a nun (you should have seen her one day pass herself off to the chaplain as a mendicant sister), or teaching the lads and girls of the vineyards to dance and sing madrigals together. The Cavaliere had a singular ingenuity in planning such entertainments, and the days were hardly long enough for their diversions. But toward the end of the summer the Duchess fell quiet and would hear only sad music, and the two sat together much in the gazebo at the end of the garden. It was there the Duke found them one day when he drove out from Vicenza in his gilt coach. He came but once or twice a year to the villa, and it was, as my grandmother said, just a part of her poor lady's ill-luck to be wearing that day the Venetian habit, which uncovered the shoulders in a way the Duke always scowled at, and her curls loose and powdered with gold. Well, the three drank chocolate in the gazebo, and what happened no one knew, except that the Duke, on taking leave, gave his cousin a seat in his carriage; but the Cavaliere never returned,

"Winter approaching, and the poor lady thus finding herself once more alone, it was surmised among her women that she must fall into a deeper depression of spirits. But far from this being the case, she displayed such cheerfulness and equanimity of humour that my grandmother, for one, was half-vexed with her for giving no more thought to the poor young man who, all this time, was eating his heart out in the house across the valley. It is true she quitted her gold-laced gowns and wore a veil over her head; but Nencia would have it she looked the lovelier for the change, and so gave the Duke greater displeasure. Certain it is that the Duke drove out oftener to the villa, and though he found his lady always engaged in some innocent pursuit, such as embroidery or music, or playing games with her young women, yet he always went away with a sour look and a whispered word to the chaplain. Now as to the chaplain, my grandmother owned there had been a time when her Grace had not handled him over-wisely. For, according to Nencia, it seems that his reverence, who seldom approached the Duchess, being buried in his library like a moust in a cheese— well, one day he made bold to appeal to her for a sum of money, a large sum, Nencia said, to buy certain tall books, a chest full of them, that a foreign pedlar had brought him ; whereupon the Duchess, who could never abide a book, breaks out at him with a laugh and a flash of her old spirit Holy Mother of God, must I have more books about me ? I was nearly smothered with them in the first year of my marriage;' and the chaplain turning red at the affront, she added : ' You may buy them and welcome, my good chaplain, if you can find the money; but as for me, I am yet seeking a way to pay for my turquoise necklace, and the statue of Daphne at the end of the bowling-green, and the Indian parrot that my black boy brought me last Michaelmas from the Bohemians—so you see I've no money to waste on trifles ;' and as he backs out awkwardly she tosses at him over her shoulder: You should pray to Saint Blandina to open the Duke's pocket!

to which he returned very quietly ; Your Excellency's suggestion is an admirable one, and I have already entreated that blessed martyr to open the Duke's understanding.'

" Thereat, Nencia said (who was standing by), the Duchess flushed wonderfully red and waved him out of the room; and then ' Quick!' she cried to my grandmother (who was too glad to run on such errands), ' Call me Antonio, the gardener's boy, to the box-garden; I've a word to say to him about the new clove-carnations. . .'

"Now I may not have told you, sir, that in the crypt under the chapel there has stood, for more generations than a man can count, a stone coffin containing a thigh-bone of the blessed Saint Blandina of Lyons, a relic offered, I've been told, by some great Duke of France to one of our own dukes when they fought the Turk together ; and the object, ever since, of particular veneration in this illustrious family. Now, since the Duchess had been left to herself, it was observed she affected a fervent devotion to this relic, praying often in the chapel and even causing the

stone slab that covered the entrance to the crypt to be replaced by a wooden one, that she might at will descend and kneel by the coffin. This was matter of edification to all the household, and should have been peculiarly pleasing to the chaplain; but, with respect to you, he was the kind of man who brings a sour mouth to the eating of the sweetest apple.

" However that may be, the Duchess, when she dismissed him, was seen running to the garden, where she talked earnestly with the boy Antonio about the new clove-carnations, and the rest of the day she sat indoors and played sweetly on the virginal. Now Nencia always had it in mind that her Grace had made a mistake in refusing that request of the chaplain's; but she said nothing, for to talk reason to the Duchess was of no more use than praying for rain in a drought.

"Winter came early that year, there was snow on the hills by All Souls, the wind stripped the gardens, and the lemon-trees were nipped in the lemon-house. The Duchess kept her room in this black season, sitting over the fire, embroidering,

reading books of devotion (which was a thing she had never done), and praying frequently in the chapel. As for the chaplain, it was a place he never set foot in but to say mass in the morning, with the Duchess overhead in the tribune, and the servants aching with rheumatism on the marble floor. The chaplain himself hated the cold, and galloped through the mass like a man with witches after him. The rest of the day he spent in his library, over a brazier, with his eternal books. . .

" You'll wonder, sir, if I'm ever to get to the gist of the story; and I've gone slowly, I own, for fear of what's coming. Well, the winter was long and hard. When it fell cold the Duke ceased to come out from Vicenza, and not a soul had the Duchess to speak to but her maid-servants and the gardeners about the place. Yet it was wonderful, my grandmother said, how she kept her brave colours and her spirits; only it was remarked that she prayed longer in the chapel, where a brazier was kept burning for her all day. When the young are denied their natural pleasures they turn often enough to religion; and it was a mercy, as my grandmother said, that she, who had scarce a live sinner to speak to, should take such comfort in a dead saint.

"My grandmother seldom saw her that winter, for though she showed a brave front to all, she kept more and more to herself, choosing to have only Nencia about her, and dismissing even her when she went to pray. For her devotion had that mark of true piety, that she wished it not to be observed; so that Nencia had strict orders, on the chaplain's approach, to warn her mistress if she happened to be in prayer.

"Well, the winter passed, and spring was well forward, when my grandmother one evening had a bad fright. That it was her own fault I won't deny, for she'd been down the lime-walk with Antonio when her aunt fancied her to be stitching in her chamber; and seeing a sudden light in Nencia's window, she took fright lest her disobedience be found out, and ran up quickly through the laurel-grove to the house. Her way lay by the chapel, and as she crept past it, meaning to slip in through the scullery, and groping her way, for the dark had fallen and the moon was scarce up, she heard a crash close behind her, as though some one had dropped from a window of the chapel. The young fool's heart turned over, but she looked round as she ran, and there, sure enough, was a man scuttling across the terrace; and as he doubled the corner of the house my grandmother swore she caught the whisk of the chaplain's skirts. Now that was a strange thing, certainly; for why should the chaplain be getting out of the chapel window when he might have passed through the door? For you may have noticed, sir, there's a door leads from the chapel into the saloon on the ground floor; the only other way out being through the Duchess's tribune.

"Well, my grandmother turned the matter over, and next time she met Antonio in the lime-walk (which, by reason of her fright, was not for some days) she laid before him what had happened; but to her surprise he only laughed and said: 'You little simpleton, he wasn't getting out of the window, he was trying to look in;' and not another word could she get from him.

"So the season moved on to Easter, and news came the Duke had gone to Rome for that holy festivity. His comings and goings made no change at the villa, and yet there was no one there but felt easier to think his yellow face was on the far side of the Apennines, unless perhaps it was the chaplain.

"Well, it was one day in May that the Duchess, who had walked long with Nencia on the terrace, rejoicing at the sweetness of the prospect and the pleasant scent of the gilly-flowers in the stone vases, the Duchess toward mid-day withdrew to her rooms, giving orders that her dinner should be served in her bedchamber. My grandmother helped to carry in the dishes, and observed, she said, the singular beauty of the Duchess, who in honour of the fine weather had put on a gown of shot-silver and hung her bare shoulders with pearls, so that she looked fit to dance at court with an emperor. She had ordered, too, a rare repast for a lady that heeded so little what she ate—jellies, game-pasties, fruits in syrup, spiced cakes and a flagon of Greek wine; and she nodded and clapped her hands as the women set it before her, saying again and again, 'I shall eat well to-day.'

"But presently another mood seized her; she turned from the table, called for her rosary, and said to Nencia; 'The fine weather has made me neglect my devotions. I must say a litany before I dine.'

"She ordered the women out and barred the door, as her custom was; and Nencia and my grandmother went downstairs to work in the linen-room.

"Now the linen-room gives on the court-yard, and suddenly my grandmother saw a strange sight approaching. First up the avenue came the Duke's carriage (whom all thought to be in Rome), and after it, drawn by a long string of mules and oxen, a cart carrying what looked like a kneeling figure wrapped in death-clothes. The strangeness of it struck the girl dumb, and the Duke's coach was at the door before she had the wit to cry out that it was coming. Nencia, when she saw it, went white and ran out of the room. My grandmother followed, scared by her face, and the two fled along the corridor to the chapel. On the way they met the chaplain, deep in a book, who asked in surprise where they were running, and when they said to announce the Duke's arrival, he fell into such astonishment, and asked them so many questions, and uttered such Ohs and Ahs, that by the time he let them by the Duke was at their heels. Nencia reached the chapel-door first, and cried out that the Duke was coming; and before she had a reply he was at her side, with the chaplain following.

" A moment later the door opened and there stood the Duchess. She held her rosary in one hand and had drawn a scarf over her shoulders; but they shone through it like the moon in a mist, and her countenance sparkled with beauty.

" The Duke took her hand with a bow.

"Madam he said, I could have had no greater happiness than thus to surprise you at your devotions.'

" My own happiness,' she replied,

" would have been greater had your Excellency prolonged it by giving me notice of your arrival.'

" Had you expected me, Madam,' said he, ' your appearance could scarcely have been more fitted to the occasion. Few ladies of your youth and beauty array themselves to venerate a saint as they would to welcome a lover.'

" Sir,' she answered, ' having never enjoyed the latter opportunity, I am constrained to make the most of the former. What's that?' she cried, falling back, and the rosary dropped from her hand.

"There was a loud noise at the other end of the saloon, as of a heavy object being dragged down the passage; and presently a dozen men were seen hauling across the threshold the shrouded thing from the ox-cart. The Duke waved his hand toward it. ' That,' said he, ' Madam, is a tribute to your extraordinary piety. I have heard, with peculiar satisfaction of your devotion to the blessed relics in this chapel, and to commemorate a zeal which neither the rigours of winter nor the sultriness of summer could abate, I have ordered a sculptured image of you, marvellously executed by the Cavaliere Bernini, to be placed before the altar over the entrance to the crypt.'

"The Duchess, who had grown pale,

I

nevertheless smiled playfully at this. ' As to commemorating my piety,' she said, ' I recognise there one of your Excellency's pleasantries

" A pleasantry?' the Duke interrupted; and he made a sign to the men, who had now reached the threshold of the chapel. In an instant the wrappings fell from the figure, and there knelt the Duchess to the life. A cry of wonder rose from all, but the Duchess herself stood whiter than the marble.

" You will see," says the Duke, this is no pleasantly, but a triumph of the incomparable Bernini's chisel. The likeness was done from your miniature portrait by the divine Elisabetta Sirani, which I sent to the master some six months ago, with what results all must admire.'

"' Six months !' cried the Duchess, and seemed about to fall; but his Excellency caught her by the hand.

" ' Nothing,' he said,' could better please me than the excessive emotion you display, for true piety is ever modest, and your thanks could not take a form that better became you. And now,' says he to the men, let the image be put in place.'

" By this, life seemed to have returned to the Duchess, and she answered him with a deep reverence. 'That I should be overcome by so unexpected a grace, your Excellency admits to be natural; but what honours you accord it is my privilege to accept, and I entreat only that in mercy to my modesty the image be placed in the remotest part of the chapel.'

" At that the Duke darkened. < What! You would have this masterpiece of a renowned chisel, which, I disguise not, cost me the price of a good vineyard in gold pieces, you would have it thrust out of sight like the work of a village stonecutter ?'

" ' It is my semblance, not the sculptor's work, I desire to conceal.'

" ' If you are fit for my house, Madam, you are fit for God's, and entitled to the place of honour in both. Bring the statue forward, you dawdlers!' he called out to the men.

" The Duchess fell back submissively. ' You are right, sir, as always ; but I would at least have the image stand on the left of the altar, that, looking up, it may behold your Excellency's seat in the tribune.'

" A pretty thought, Madam, for which I thank you; but I design before long to put my companion image on the other side of the altar; and the wife's place, as you know, is at her husband's right hand.'

" True, my Lord—but, again, if my poor presentment is to have the unmerited honour of kneeling beside yours, why not place both before the altar, where it is our habit to pray in life ?'

" ' And where, Madam, should we kneel if they took our places ? Besides,' says the Duke, still speaking very blandly, * I have a more particular purpose in placing your image over the entrance to the crypt; for not only would I thereby mark your special devotion to the blessed saint who rests there, but, by sealing up the opening in the pavement, would assure the perpetual preservation of that holy martyr's bones, which hitherto have been too thoughtlessly exposed to sacrilegious attempts.'

" ' What attempts, my Lord ?' cries the Duchess. ' No one enters this chapel without my leave.'

"' So I have understood, and can well believe from what I have learned of your c
piety; yet at night a malefactor might break in through a window, Madam, and your Excellency not know it.'

" ' I'm a light sleeper,' said the Duchess.

"The Duke looked at her gravely. ' Indeed ?' said he. ' A bad sign at your age. I must see that you are provided with a sleeping-draught.'

"The Duchess's eyes filled. 'You would deprive me, then, of the consolation of visiting those venerable relics ?'

" ' I would have you keep eternal guard over them, knowing no one to whose care they may more fittingly be entrusted.'

" By this the image was brought close to the wooden slab that covered the entrance to the crypt, when the Duchess, springing forward, placed herself in the way.

"' Sir, let the statue be put in place to-morrow, and suffer me, to-night, to say a last prayer beside those holy bones.'

"The Duke stepped instantly to her side. ' Well thought, Madam ; I will go down with you now, and we will pray together.'

"' Sir, your long absences have, alas! given me the habit of solitary devotion, and I confess that any presence is distracting

"' Madam, I accept your rebuke. Hitherto, it is true, the duties of my station have constrained me to long absences; but henceforward I remain with you while you live. Shall we go down into the crypt together ?'

" ' No; for I fear for your Excellency's ague. The air there is excessively damp.'

"'The more reason you should no longer be exposed to it; and to prevent the intemperance of your zeal I will at once make the place inaccessible.'

" The Duchess at this fell on her knees on the slab, weeping excessively and lifting her hands to Heaven.

" ' Oh,' she cried, ' you are cruel, sir, to deprive me of access to the sacred relics that have enabled me to support with resignation the solitude to which your Excellency's duties have condemned me; and if prayer and meditation give me any authority to pronounce on such matters, suffer me to warn you, sir, that I fear the blessed Saint Blandina will punish us for thus abandoning her venerable remains 1 '

" The Duke at this seemed to pause, for he was a pious man, and my grandmother thought she saw him exchange a glance with the chaplain; who, stepping timidly forward, with his eyes on the ground, said : 'There is indeed much wisdom in her Excellency's words, but I would suggest, sir, that her pious wish might be met, and the saint more conspicuously honoured, by transferring the relics from the crypt to a place beneath the altar.'

" < True!' cried the Duke, ' and it shall be done at once.'

" But thereat the Duchess rose to her feet with a terrible look.

"' No,' she cried, < by the body of God ! For it shall not be said that, after your Excellency has chosen to deny every request I addressed to him, I owe his consent to the solicitation of another!'

" The chaplain turned red and the Duke yellow, and for a moment neither spoke.

" Then the Duke said, ' Here are words enough, Madam. Do you wish the relics brought up from the crypt ?'

" (I wish nothing that 1 owe to another's intervention!'

" ' Put the image in place then,' says the Duke furiously; and handed her Grace to a chair.

"She sat there, my grandmother said, straight as an arrow, her hands locked, her head high, her eyes on the Duke, while the statue was dragged to its place; then she stood up and turned away. As she passed by Nencia, ' Call me Antonio,' she whispered ; but before the words were out of her mouth the Duke stepped between them.

"'Madam,' says he, all smiles now, ' I have travelled straight from Rome to bring you the sooner this proof of my esteem. I lay last night at Monselice, and have been on the road since daybreak. Will you not invite me to supper?'

"'Surely, my Lord,' said the Duchess. 'It shall be laid in the dining-parlour within the hour.'

"'Why not in your chamber and at once, Madam? Since I believe it is your custom to sup there.'

"'In my chamber?' says the Duchess, in disorder.

"'Have you anything against it?' he asked.

"'Assuredly not, sir, if you will give me time to prepare myself.'

"'I will wait in your cabinet,' said the Duke.

"At that, said my grandmother, the Duchess gave one look, as the souls in hell may have looked when the gates closed on our Lord; then she called Nencia and passed to her chamber.

"What happened there my grandmother could never learn, but that the Duchess, in great haste, dressed herself with extraordinary splendour, powdering her hair with gold, painting her face and bosom, and covering herself with jewels till she shone like our Lady of Loretto; and hardly were these preparations complete when the Duke entered from the cabinet, followed by the servants carrying supper. Thereupon the Duchess dismissed Nencia, and what follows my grandmother learned from a pantry-lad who brought up the dishes and waited in the cabinet; for only the Duke's body-servant entered the bed chamber.

"Well, according to this boy, sir, who was looking and listening with his whole body, as it were, because he had never

before been suffered so near the Duchess, it appears that the noble couple sat down in great good humour, the Duchess playfully reproving her husband for his long absence, while the Duke swore that to look so beautiful was the best way of punishing him. In this tone the talk continued, with such gay sallies on the part of the Duchess, such tender advances on the Duke's, that the lad declared they were for all the world like a pair of lovers courting on a summer's night in the vineyard; and so it went till the servant brought in the mulled wine.

"'Ah,' the Duke was saying at that moment, 'this agreeable evening repays me for the many dull ones I have spent away from you; nor do I remember to have enjoyed such laughter since the afternoon last year when we drank chocolate in the gazebo with my cousin Ascanio. And that reminds me,' he said, 'is my cousin in good health?'

"'I have no reports of it,' says the Duchess. 'But your Excellency should taste these figs stewed in malmsey'

"'I am in the mood to taste whatever you offer,' said he; and as she helped him to the figs, he added, 'if my enjoyment were not complete as it is, I could almost wish my cousin Ascanio were with us. The fellow is rare good company at supper. What do you say, Madam? I hear he's still in the country; shall we send for him to join us?'

"'Ah,' said the Duchess, with a sigh and a languishing look, 'I see your Excellency wearies of me already.'

"'Madam? Ascanio is a capital good fellow, but to my mind his chief merit at this moment is his absence. It inclines me so tenderly to him that, by God, I could empty a glass to his good health.'

"With that the Duke caught up his goblet and signed to the servant to fill the Duchess's.

"'Here's to the cousin,' he cried, standing, 'who has the good taste to stay away when he's not wanted. I drink to his very long life and you, Madam?'

"At this the Duchess, who had sat staring at him with a changed face, rose also and lifted her glass to her lips.

"'And I to his happy death,' says she in a wild voice; and as she spoke the empty goblet dropped from her hand and she fell face down on the floor.

"The Duke shouted to her women that she had swooned, and they came and lifted her to the bed. . . She suffered horribly all night, Nencia said, twisting herself like a heretic at the stake, but without a word escaping her. The Duke watched by her, and toward daylight sent for the chaplain; but by this she was unconscious, and, her teeth being locked, our Lord's body could not be passed through them.

"The Duke announced to his relations that his lady had died after partaking too freely of spiced wine and an omelet of carp's roe, at a supper she had prepared in honour of his return; and the next year he brought home a new Duchess, who gave him a son and five daughters. . ."

THE sky had turned to a steel grey, against which the villa stood out sallow and inscrutable. A wind strayed through the gardens, loosening here and there a yellow leaf from the sycamores; and the hills across the valley were purple as thunder clouds.

"And the statue?" I asked.

"Ah, the statue. Well, sir, this is what my grandmother told me, here on this very bench where we're sitting. The poor child, who worshipped the Duchess as a girl of her years will worship a beautiful kind mistress, spent a night of horror, you may fancy, shut out from her lady's room, hearing the cries that came from it, and seeing, as she crouched in her corner, the women rush to and fro with wild looks, the Duke's lean face in the door, and the chaplain skulking in the antechamber with his eyes on his breviary. No one minded her that night or the next morning; and toward dusk, when it became known the Duchess was no more, the poor girl felt the pious wish to say a prayer for her dead mistress. She crept to the chapel and stole in unobserved. The place was empty and dim, but as she advanced she heard a low moaning, and coming in front of the statue she saw that its face, the day before so sweet and smiling, had the look on it that you know — and the moaning seemed to come from its lips. My grandmother turned cold, but something she said afterward, kept her from calling or shrieking out, and she turned and ran from the place. In the passage she fell in a swoon; and when she came to her senses, in her own chamber, she heard that the Duke had locked the chapel door and forbidden any to set foot there. . . . The place was never opened again till the Duke died, some ten years later; and then it was that the other servants, going in with the new heir, saw for the first time the horror that my grandmother had kept in her bosom. . . ."

"And the crypt?" I asked. "Has it never been opened?"

"Heaven forbid, sir!" cried the old man, crossing himself. "Was it not the Duchess's express wish that the relics should not be disturbed?"

THE ANGEL AT THE GRAVE

THE ANGEL AT THE GRAVE

THE House stood a few yards back from the elm-shaded village street, in that semi-publicity sometimes cited as a democratic protest against old-world standards of domestic exclusiveness. This candid exposure to the public eye is more probably a result of the gregariousness which, in New England bosom, oddly co-exists with a shrinking from direct social contact; most of the inmates of such houses preferring that furtive intercourse which is the result of observations through shuttered windows and a categorical acquaintance with the neighbouring clothes-lines. The House, however, faced its public with a difference. For sixty years it had written itself with a capital letter, had self-consciously squared itself in the eye of an admiring nation. The most searching inroads of village intimacy hardly counted in a household that opened on the universe; and a lady whose door bell was at any moment liable to be rung by visitors from London or Vienna was not likely to flutter upstairs when she observed a neighbour " stepping over."

The solitary inmate of the Anson House owed this induration of the social texture to the most conspicuous accident in her annals: the fact that she was the only grand-daughter of the great Orestes Anson. She had been born, as it were, into a museum, and cradled in a glass case with a label; the first foundations of her consciousness being built on the rock of her grandfather's celebrity. To a little girl who acquires her earliest knowledge of literature through a Reader embellished with fragments of her ancestor's prose, that personage necessarily fills an heroic space in the foreground of life. To communicate with one's past through the impressive medium of print, to have, as it were, a footing in every library in the country, and an acknow-ledged kinship with that world-diffused clan, the descendants of the great, was to be pledged to a standard of manners that amazingly simplified the lesser relations of life. The village street on which Paulina Anson's youth looked out led to all the capitals of Europe; and over the roads of intercommunication unseen caravans bore back to the elm-shaded House the tribute of an admiring world.

Fate seemed to have taken a direct share in fitting Paulina for her part as the custodian of this historic dwelling. It had long been secretly regarded as a "visitation" by the great man's family that he had left no son and that his daughters were not "intellectual." The ladies themselves were the first to lament their deficiency, to own that nature had denied them the gift of making the most of their opportunities. A profound veneration for their parent and an unswerving faith in his doctrines had not amended their congenital incapacity to understand what he had written. Laura, who had her moments of mute rebellion against destiny, had sometimes thought D how much easier it would have been if their progenitor had been a poet; for she could recite, with feeling, portions of The Culprit Fay and of the poems of Mrs Hemans; and Phoebe, who was more conspicuous for memory than imagination, kept an album filled with " selections." But the great man was a philosopher; and to both daughters respiration was difficult on the cloudy heights of meta-physic. The situation would have been intolerable but for the fact that, while Phoebe and Laura were still at school, their father's fame had passed from the open ground of conjecture to the chill privacy of certitude. Dr Anson had in fact achieved one of those anticipated immortalities not uncommon at a time when people were apt to base their literary judgments on their emotions, and when to affect plain food and despise England went a long way toward establishing a man's intellectual preeminence. Thus, when the daughters were called on to strike a filial attitude about their parent's pedestal, there was little to do but to pose gracefully and point upward; and there are spines to which the immobility of worship is not a strain. A legend had by this time crystallized about the great Orestes, and it was of more immediate interest to the public to hear what brand of tea he drank, and whether he took off his boots in the hall, than to rouse the drowsy echo of his dialectic. A great man never draws so near his public as when it has become unnecessary to read his books and is still interesting to know what he eats for breakfast.

As recorders of their parent's domestic habits, as pious scavengers of his waste-paper basket, the Misses Anson were unexcelled. They always had an interesting anecdote to impart to the literary pilgrim, and the tact with which, in later years, they intervened between the public and the growing inaccessibility of its idol, sent away many an enthusiast satisfied to have touched the veil before the sanctuary. Still it was felt, especially by old Mrs Anson, who survived her husband for some years, that Phoebe and Laura were not worthy of their privileges. There had been a third daughter so unworthy of hers that she had married

a distant cousin, who had taken her to live in a new western community where the Works of Orestes Anson had not yet become a part of the civic consciousness; but of this daughter little was said, and she was tacitly understood to be excluded from the family heritage of fame. In time, however, it appeared that the traditional penny with which she had been cut off had been invested to unexpected advantage; and the interest on it, when she died, returned to the Anson House in the shape of a grand-daughter, who was at once felt to be what Mrs Anson called a " compensation." It was Mrs Anson's firm belief that the remotest operations of nature were governed by the centripetal force of her husband's greatness, and that Paulina's exceptional intelligence could be explained only on the ground that she was designed to act as the guardian of the family temple.

The House, by the time Paulina came to live in it, had already acquired the publicity of a place of worship; not the perfumed chapel of a romantic idolatry, but the cold, clean, empty meeting-house of ethical enthusiasms. The ladies lived

on its outskirts, as it were, in cells that left the central fane undisturbed. The very position of the furniture had come to have a ritual significance: the sparse ornaments were the offerings of kindred intellects, the steel engravings by Raphael Morghen marked the Via Sacra of a European tour, and the black-walnut desk with its bronze inkstand modelled on the Pantheon was the altar of this bleak temple of thought.

To a child compact of enthusiasms, and accustomed to pasture them on the scanty herbage of a new social soil, the atmosphere of the old house was full of floating nourishment. In the compressed perspective of Paulina's outlook it stood for a monument of ruined civilizations, and its white portico opened on legendary distances. Its very aspect was impressive to eyes that had first surveyed life from the jig-saw " residence" of a raw-edged western town. The high-ceilinged rooms, with their panelled walls, their polished mahogany, their portraits of triple-stocked ancestors and of ringleted " females " in crayon, furnished the child with the historic scenery against which a

young imagination constructs its vision of the past. To other eyes the cold, spotless, thinly-furnished interior might have suggested the shuttered mind of a maiden-lady who associates fresh air and sunlight with dust and discoloration; but it is the eye which supplies the colouring-matter, and Paulina's brimmed with the richest hues.

Nevertheless, the House did not immediately dominate her. She had her confused out-reachings toward other centres of sensation, her vague intuition of a heliocentric system; but the attraction of habit, the steady pressure of example, gradually fixed her roving allegiance and she bent her neck to the yoke. Vanity had a share in her subjugation; for it had early been discovered that she was the only person in the family who could read her grandfather's works. The fact that she had perused them with delight at an age when (even presupposing a metaphysical bias) it was impossible for her to understand them, seemed to her aunts and grandmother sure evidence of predestination. Paulina was to be the interpreter of the oracle, and the philosophic fumes so vertiginous to meaner minds would throw her into the needed condition of clairvoyance. Nothing could have been more genuine than the emotion on which this theory was based. Paulina, in fact, delighted in her grandfather's writings. His sonorous periods, his mystic vocabulary, his bold flights into the rarefied air of the abstract, were thrilling to a fancy unhampered by the need of definitions. This purely verbal pleasure was supplemented later by the excitement of gathering up crumbs of meaning from the rhetorical board. What could have been more stimulating than to construct the theory of a girlish world out of the fragments of this Titanic cosmogony ? Before Paulina's opinions had reached the stage when ossification sets in, their form was fatally predetermined.

The fact that Dr Anson had died, and that his apotheosis had taken place before his young priestess's induction to the temple, made her ministrations easier and more inspiring. There were no little personal traits—such as the great man's manner of helping himself to salt, or the guttural cluck that started the wheels of speech—to distract the eye of young veneration from the central fact of his divinity. A man whom one knows only through a crayon portrait and a dozen yellowing tomes on free-will and intuition is at least secure from the belittling effects of intimacy.

Paulina thus grew up in a world readjusted to the fact of her grandfather's greatness; and as each organism draws from its surroundings the kind of nourishment most needful to its growth, so from this somewhat colourless conception she absorbed warmth, brightness, and variety. Paulina was the type of woman who transmutes thought into sensation and nurses a theory in her bosom like a child.

In due course Mrs Anson "passed away "—no one died in the Anson vocabulary—and Paulina became more than ever the foremost figure of the commemorative group. Laura and Phoebe, content to leave their father's glory in more competent hands, placidly lapsed into needlework and fiction, and their niece stepped into immediate prominence as the chief "authority" on the great man. Historians who were " getting up " the period wrote to consult her and to borrow documents ; ladies with inexplicable yearnings begged for an interpretation of phrases which had " influenced " them, but which they had not quite understood ; critics applied to her to verify some doubtful citation or to decide some disputed point in chronology ; and the great tide of thought and investigation kept up a continuous murmur on the quiet shores of her life.

An explorer of another kind disembarked there one day in the shape of a young man, to whom Paulina was primarily a kissable girl, with an afterthought in the shape of a grandfather. From the outset it had been impossible to fix Hewlett Winsloe's attention on Dr Anson. The young man behaved with the innocent profanity of infants sporting on a tomb. His excuse was that he came from New York, a Cimmerian outskirt which survived in Paulina's geography only because Dr Anson had gone there once or twice to lecture. The curious thing was that she should have thought it worth while to find excuses for young Winsloe. The fact that she did so had not escaped the attention of the village; but people, after a gasp of awe, said it was the most natural thing in the world that a girl like Paulina Anson should think of marrying. It would certainly seem a little odd to see a man in the House, but young Winsloe would of course understand that the doctor's books were not to be disturbed, and that he must go down to the orchard to smoke . The village had barely framed this modus vivendi when it was convulsed by the announcement that young Winsloe declined to live in the House on any terms. Hang going down to the orchard to smoke ! He meant to take his wife to New York. The village drew its breath and watched.

Did Persephone, snatched from the warm fields of Enna, peer half-consent-ingly down the abyss that opened at her feet? Paulina, it must be owned, hung a moment over the black gulf of temptation. She would have found it easy to cope with a deliberate disregard of her grandfather's rights ; but young Winsloe's unconsciousness of that shadowy claim was as much a natural function as the falling of leaves on a grave. His love was an embodiment of the perpetual renewal which to some tender spirits seems a crueller process than decay.

On women of Paulina's mould this piety toward implicit demands, toward the ghosts of dead duties walking un-appeased among usurping passions, has a stronger hold than any tangible bond. People said that she gave up young Winsloe because her aunts disapproved of her leaving them ; but such disapproval as reached her was an emanation from the walls of the House, from the bare desk, the faded portraits, the dozen yellowing tomes that no hand but hers ever lifted from the shelf.

AFTER that the House possessed her. As if conscious of its victory, it imposed a conqueror's claims. It had once been suggested that she should write a life of her grandfather, and the task from which she had shrunk as from a too-oppressive privilege now shaped itself into a justification of her course. In a burst of filial pantheism she tried to lose herself in the vast ancestral consciousness. Her one refuge from scepticism was a blind faith in the magnitude and the endurance of the idea to which she had sacrificed her life, and with a passionate instinct of self-preservation she laboured to fortify her position.

The preparations for the Life led her through byways that the most scrupulous of the previous biographers had left unexplored. She accumulated her material with a blind animal patience unconscious of fortuitous risks. The years stretched before her like some vast blank page spread out to receive the record of her toil; and she had a mystic conviction that she would not die till her work was accomplished.

The aunts, sustained by no such high purpose, withdrew in turn to their respective divisions of the Anson " plot," and Paulina remained alone with her task. She was forty when the book was completed. She had travelled little in her life, aud it had become more and more difficult to her to leave the House even for a day; but the dread of entrusting her document to a strange hand made her decide to cariy it herself to the publisher. On the way to Boston she had a sudden vision of the loneliness to which this last parting condemned her. All her youth, all her dreams, all her renunciations lay in that neat bundle on her knee. It was not so much her grandfather's life as her own that she had written; and the knowledge that it would come back to her in all the glorification of print was of no more help than to a mother's grief, the assurance that the lad she must part with will return with epaulets.

She had naturally addressed herself to the firm which had published her grandfather's works. Its founder, a personal friend of the philosopher's, had survived the Olympian group, of which he had been a subordinate member, long enough to bestow his octogenarian approval on Paulina's pious undertaking. But he had died soon afterward; and Miss Anson found herself confronted by his grandson, a person with a brisk commercial view of his trade, who was said to have put " new blood " into the firm.

This gentleman listened attentively, fingering her manuscript as though literature were a tactile substance; then, with a confidential twist of his revolving chair, he emitted the verdict: "We ought to have had this ten years sooner."

Miss Anson took the words as an allusion to the repressed avidity of her readers. " It has been a long time for the public to wait," she solemnly assented.

The publisher smiled. " They haven't waited," he said.

She looked at him strangely. " Haven't waited ? "

"No—they've gone off; taken another train. Literature's like a big railway-station now, you know: there's a train starting every minute. People are not going to hang round the waiting-room. If they can't get to a place when they want to, they go somewhere else."

The application of this parable cost Miss Anson several minutes of throbbing silence. At length she said: "Then I am to understand that the public is no longer interested in— in my grandfather ?" She felt as though Heaven must blast the lips that risked such a conjecture.

" Well, it's this way. He's a name still, of course. People don't exactly want to be caught not knowing who he is; but they don't want to spend two dollars finding out, when they can look him up for nothing in any biographical dictionary."

Miss Anson's world reeled. She felt herself adrift among mysterious forces, and no more thought of prolonging the discussion than of opposing an earthquake with argument. She went home carrying the manuscript like a wounded thing. On the return journey she found herself travelling straight toward a fact that had lurked for months in the background of her life, and that now seemed to await her on the very threshold : the fact that fewer visitors came to the House. She owned to herself that for the last four or five years the number had steadily diminished. Engrossed in her work, she had noted the change only to feel thankful that she had fewer interruptions. There had been a time when, at the travelling season, the bell rang continuously, and the ladies of the House lived in a chronic state of "best silks" and expectancy. It would have been im-

possible then to carry on any consecutive work; and she now saw that the silence which had gathered round her task had been the hush of death.

Not of his death! The very walls cried out against the implication. It was the world's enthusiasm, the world's faith, the world's loyalty that had died. A corrupt generation that had turned aside to worship the brazen serpent. Her heart yearned with a prophetic passion over the lost sheep straying in the wilderness. But all great glories had their interlunar period; and in due time her grandfather would once more flash full-orbed upon a darkling world.

The few friends to whom she confided her adventure reminded her with tender indignation that there were other publishers less subject to the fluctuations of the market; but much as she had braved for her grandfather she could not again brave that particular probation. She found herself, in fact, incapable of any immediate effort. She had lost her way in a labyrinth of conjecture where her worst dread was that she might put her hand upon the clue.

She locked up the manuscript and sat down to wait. If a pilgrim had come just then the priestess would have fallen on his neck; but she continued to celebrate her rites alone. It was a double solitude; for she had always thought a great deal more of the people who came to see the House than of the people who came to see her. She fancied that the neighbours kept a keen eye on the path to the House; and there were days when the figure of a stranger strolling past the gate seemed to focus upon her the scorching sympathies of the village. For a time she thought of travelling; of going to Europe, or even to Boston ; but to leave the House now would have seemed like deserting her post. Gradually her scattered energies centred themselves in the fierce resolve to understand what had happened. She was not the woman to live long in an unmapped country, or to accept as final her private interpretation of phenomena. Like a traveller, in unfamiliar regions, she began to store for future guidance the minutest natural signs. Unflinchingly she noted the accumulating symptoms of indifference that marked her grandfather's

descent toward posterity. She passed from the heights on which he had been grouped with the sages of his day to the lower level where he had come to be " the friend of Emerson, the correspondent of Hawthorne," or (later still) "the Dr Anson " mentioned in their letters. The change had taken place as slowly and imperceptibly as a natural process. She could not say that any ruthless hand had stripped the leaves from the tree: it was simply that, among the evergreen glories of his group, her grandfather's had proved deciduous.

She had still to ask herself why. If the decay had been a natural process, was it not the very pledge of renewal ? It was easier to find such arguments than to be convinced by them. Again and again she tried to drug her solitude with analogies; but at last she saw that such expedients were but the expression of a growing incredulity. The best way of proving her faith in her grandfather was not to be afraid of his critics. She had no notion where these shadowy antagonists lurked; for she had never heard of the great man's doctrine being directly

combated. Oblique assaults there must have been, however, Parthian shots at the giant that none dared face; and she thirsted to close with such assailants. The difficulty was to find them. She began by re-reading the Works; thence she passed to the writers of the same school, those whose rhetoric bloomed perennial in First Readers from which her grandfather's prose had long since faded. Amid that clamour of far-off enthusiasms she detected no controversial note. The little knot of Olympians held their views in common with an early Christian promiscuity. They were continually proclaiming their admiration for each other, the public joining as chorus in this guileless antiphon of praise ; and she discovered no traitor in their midst.

What then had happened ? Was it simply that the main current of thought had set another way ? Then why did the others survive ? Why were they still marked down as tributaries to the philosophic stream ? This question carried her still farther afield, and she pressed on with the passion of a champion whose reluctance to know the worst might be con-

strued into a doubt of his cause. At length — slowly but inevitably — an explanation shaped itself. Death had overtaken the doctrines about which her grandfather had draped his cloudy rhetoric. They had disintegrated and been re-absorbed, adding their little pile to the dust drifted about the mute lips of the sphinx. The great man's contemporaries had survived not by reason of what they taught, but of what they were; and he, who had been the mere mask through which they mouthed their lesson, the instrument on which their tune was played, lay buried deep among the obsolete tools of thought.

The discovery came to Paulina suddenly. She looked up one evening from her reading and it stood before her like a ghost. It had entered her life with stealthy steps, creeping close before she was aware of it. She sat in the library, among the carefully-tended books and portraits; and it seemed to her that she had been walled alive into a tomb hung with the effigies of dead ideas. She felt a desperate longing to escape into the outer air, where people toiled and loved, and living sympathies went hand in hand. It was the sense of wasted labour that oppressed her; of two lives consumed in that ruthless process that uses generations of effort to build a single cell. There was a dreary parallel between her grandfather's fruitless toil and her own unprofitable sacrifice. Each in turn had kept vigil by a corpse.

in

THE bell rang—she remembered it afterward—with a loud thrilling note. It was what they used to call the " visitor's ring "; not the tentative tinkle of a neighbour dropping in to borrow a saucepan or discuss parochial incidents, but a decisive summons from the outer world.

Miss Anson put down her knitting and listened. She sat upstairs now, making her rheumatism an excuse for avoiding the rooms below. Her interests had insensibly adjusted themselves to the perspective of her neighbours' lives, and she wondered—as the bell re-echoed—if it could mean that Mrs Heminway's baby had come. Conjecture had time to ripen into certainty, and she was limping toward the closet where her cloak and bonnet hung, when her little maid fluttered in with the announcement: "A gentleman to see the house."

" The House "

"Yes, m'm. I don't know what he means," faltered the messenger, whose memory did not embrace the period when such announcements were a daily part of the domestic routine.

Miss Anson glanced at the proffered card. The name it bore— Mr George Corby —was unknown to her, but the blood rose to her languid cheek. " Hand me my Mechlin cap, Katie," she said, trembling a little, as she laid aside her walking-stick. She put her cap on before the mirror, with rapid unsteady touches. " Did you draw up the library blinds ?" she breathlessly asked.

She had gradually built up a wall of commonplace between herself and her illusions, but at the first summons of the past filial passion swept away the frail barriers of expediency.

She walked downstairs so hurriedly that her stick clicked like a girlish heel; but in the hall she paused, wondering nervously if Katie had put a match to the fire. The autumn air was cold, and she had the reproachful vision of a visitor with elderly ailments shivering by her inhospitable hearth. She thought instinctively of the stranger as a survivor of the days when such a visit was a part of the young enthusiast's itinerary.

The fire was unlit, and the room forbiddingly cold; but the figure which, as Miss Anson entered, turned from a lingering scrutiny of the bookshelves, was that of a fresh-eyed sanguine youth clearly independent of any artificial caloric. She stood still a moment, feeling herself the victim of some anterior impression that made this robust presence an unsubstantial thing; but the young man advanced with an air of genial assurance which rendered him at once more real and more reminiscent.

" Why this, you know," he exclaimed, " is simply immense!"

The words, which did not immediately present themselves as slang to Miss Anson's unaccustomed ear, echoed with an odd familiarity through the academic silence.

"The room, you know, I mean," he explained with a comprehensive gesture. " These jolly portraits, and the books—that's the old gentleman himself over the mantelpiece, I suppose?—and the elms outside, and—and the whole business. I do like a congruous background—don't you ? "

His hostess was silent. No one but Hewlett Winsloe had ever spoken of her grandfather as the " old gentleman."

" It's a hundred times better than I could have hoped," her visitor continued, with a cheerful disregard of her silence. " The seclusion, the remoteness, the philosophic atmosphere—there's so little of that kind of flavour left! I should have simply hated to find that he lived over a grocery, you know. I had the deuce of a time finding out where he did live," he began again, after finding another glance of parenthetical enjoyment. " But finally I got on the trail through some old book on Brook Farm. I was bound I'd get the environment right before I did my article."

Miss Anson, by this time, had recovered sufficient self-possession to seat herself and assign a chair to her visitor.

" Do I understand," she asked slowly, following his rapid eye about the room, " that you intend to write an article about my grandfather ?"

" That's what I'm here for," Mr Corby genially responded; " that is, if you're willing to help me; for I can't get on without your help," he added with a confident smile.

There was another pause, during which Miss Anson noticed a fleck of dust on the faded leather of the writing-table and a fresh spot of discoloration in the right-hand upper corner of Raphael Morghen's " Parnassus."

"Then you believe in him?" she said, looking up. She could not tell what had prompted her; the words rushed out irresistibly.

" Believe in him ? " Corby cried, springing to his feet. "Believe in Orestes Anson ? Why, I believe he's simply the greatest—the most stupendous—the most phenomenal figure we've got!"

The colour rose to Miss Anson's brow. Her heart was beating passionately. She kept her eyes fixed on the young man's face, as though it might vanish if she looked away.

" You—you mean to say this in your article ?" she asked.

" Say it ? Why, the facts will say it," he exulted. "The baldest kind of a statement would make it clear. When a man is as big as that he doesn't need a pedestal!"

Miss Anson sighed. "People used to say that when I was young," she murmured. " But now "

Her visitor stared. " When you were young ? But how did they know—when the thing hung fire as it did? When the whole edition was thrown back on his hands ?"

"The whole edition—what edition?" It was Miss Anson's turn to stare.

" Why, of his pamphlet— the pamphlet —the one thing that counts, that survives, that makes him what he is ! For Heaven's sake," he tragically adjured her, "don't tell me there isn't a copy of it left!"

Miss Anson was trembling slightly. " I don't think I understand what you mean," she faltered, less bewildered by his vehemence than by the strange sense of coming on an unexplored region in the very heart of her dominion.

" Why, his account of the amphioxus, of course! You can't mean that his family didn't know about it—that you don't know about it? I came across it by the merest accident myself, in a letter of vindication that he wrote in 1830 to an old scientific paper; but I understood there were journals—early journals ; there must be references to it somewhere in the 'twenties. He must have been at least ten or twelve years ahead of Yarrell; and he saw the whole significance of it, too— he saw where it led to. As I understand it, he actually anticipated in his pamphlet Saint Hilaire's theory of the universal type, and supported the hypothesis by describing the notochord of the amphioxus as a cartilaginous vertebral column. The specialists of the day jeered at him, of course, as the specialists in Goethe's time jeered at the plant-metamorphosis. As far as I can make out, the anatomists and zoologists were down on Dr Anson to a man; that was why his cowardly publishers went back on their bargain.

But the pamphlet must be here somewhere—he writes as though, in his first disappointment, he had destroyed the whole edition; but surely there must be at least one copy left ?"

His scientific jargon was as bewildering as his slang; and there were even moments in his discourse when Miss Anson ceased to distinguish between them; but the suspense with which he continued to gaze on her acted as a challenge to her scattered thoughts.

" The amphioxus" she murmured, half-rising. " It's an animal, isn't it—a fish ? Yes, I think I remember." She sank back with the inward look of one who retraces some lost line of association.

Gradually the distance cleared, the details started into life. In her researches for the biography she had patiently followed every ramification of her subject, and one of these overgrown paths now led her back to the episode in question. The great Orestes's title of "Doctor" had in fact not been merely the spontaneous tribute of a national admiration; he had actually studied medicine in his youth, and his diaries, as his grand-daughter now recalled, showed that he had passed through a brief phase of anatomical ardour before his attention was diverted to supersensual problems. It had indeed seemed to Paulina, as she scanned those early pages, that they revealed a spontaneity, a freshness of feeling somehow absent from his later lucubrations—as though this one emotion had reached him directly, the others through some intervening medium. In the excess of her commemorative zeal she had even struggled through the unintelligible pamphlet to which a few lines in the journal had bitterly directed her. But the subject and the phraseology were alien to her and unconnected with her conception of the great man's genius; and after a hurried perusal she had averted her thoughts from the episode as from a revelation of failure. At length she rose a little unsteadily, supporting herself against the writing-table. She looked hesitatingly about the room; then she drew a key from her old-fashioned reticule and unlocked a drawer beneath one of the bookcases. Young Corby watched her breathlessly. With a tremulous hand she turned over the dusty documents that seemed to fill the drawer. " Is this it?" she said, holding out a thin discoloured volume.

He seized it with a gasp. "Oh, by George," he said, dropping into the nearest chair.

She stood observing him strangely as his eye devoured the mouldy pages.

" Is this the only copy left ?" he asked at length, looking up for a moment as a thirsty man lifts his head from his glass.

" I think it must be. I found it long ago, among some old papers that my aunts were burning up after my grandmother's death. They said it was of no use—that he'd always meant to destroy the whole edition, and that I ought to respect his wishes. But it was something he had written; to burn it was like shutting the door against his voice— against something he had once wished to say, and that nobody had listened to. I wanted him to feel that I was always here, ready to listen, even when others hadn't thought it worth while ; and so I kept the pamphlet, meaning to carry out his wish and destroy it before my death."

Her visitor gave a groan of retrospective anguish. " And but for me— but for to-day—you would have ? "

" I should have thought it my duty."

"Oh, by George—by George," he repeated, subdued afresh by the inadequacy of speech.

She continued to watch him in silence. At length he jumped up and impulsively caught her by both hands.

"He's bigger and bigger!" he almost shouted. "He simply leads the field! You'll help me go to the bottom of this, won't you? We must turn out all the papers — letters, journals, memoranda. He must have made notes. He must have left some record of what led up to this. We must leave nothing unexplored. By Jove!" he cried, looking up at her with his bright convincing smile, " do you know you're the grand-daughter of a Great Man ?"

Her colour flickered like a girl's. " Are you—sure of him?" she whispered, as though putting him on his guard against a possible betrayal of trust.

"Sure! Sure! My dear lady " he
measured her again with his quick confident glance. " Don't you believe in him ? "

She drew back with a confused murmur. " I—used to." She had left her hands in his: their pressure seemed to send a warm current to her heart. " It ruined my life!" she cried with sudden passion. He looked at her perplexedly.

" I gave up everything," she went on wildly, "to keep him alive. I sacrificed myself—others—I nursed his glory in my bosom and it died—and left me—left me here alone." She paused and gathered her courage with a gasp. "Don't make the same mistake !" she warned him.

He shook his head, still smiling. " No danger of that! You're not alone, my dear lady. He's here with you—he's come back to you to-day. Don't you see what's happened? Don't you see that it's your love that has kept him alive ? If you'd abandoned your post for an instant—let things pass into other hands — if your wonderful tenderness hadn't perpetually kept guard — this might have been — must have been-irretrievably lost." He laid his hand on

the pamphlet. " And then — then he would have been dead !"

"Oh!" she said, "don't tell me too suddenly!" And she turned away and sank into a chair.

The young man stood watching her in an awed silence. For a long time she sat motionless, with her face hidden, and he thought she must be weeping.

At length he said, almost shyly: " You'll let me come back, then ? You'll help me work this thing out ?"

She rose calmly and held out her hand. " I'll help you," she declared.

"I'll come to-morrow, then. Can we get to work early ?"

" As early as you please."

"At eight o'clock, then," he said briskly. " You'll have the papers ready ?"

" I'll have everything ready." She added with a half-playful hesitancy: " And the fire shall be lit for you."

He went out with his bright nod. She walked to the window and watched his buoyant figure hastening down the elm-shaded street. When she turned back into the empty room she looked as though youth had touched her on the lips.

THE RECOVERY

THE RECOVERY

the visiting stranger, Hillbridge's first question was, " Have you seen Keniston's things ? "

Keniston took precedence of the Colonial State House, the Gilbert Stuart Washington, and the Ethnological Museum; nay, he ran neck and neck with the President of the University, a pre-historic relic who had known Emerson, and who was still sent about the country in cotton-wool to open educational institutions with a toothless oration on Brook Farm.

Keniston was sent about the country too: he opened art exhibitions, laid the foundation of academies, and acted in a general sense as the spokesman and apologist of art. Hillbridge was proud of him in his peripatetic character, but his

fellow-townsmen let it be understood that to "know" Keniston one must come to Hillbridge. Never was work more dependent for its effect on "atmosphere," on milieu. Hillbridge was Keniston's milieu, and there was one lady, a devotee of his art, who went so far as to assert that once, at an exhibition in New York, she had passed a Keniston without recognizing it. " It simply didn't want to be seen in such surroundings; it was hiding itself under an incognito," she declared.

It was a source of special pride to Hill-bridge that it contained all the artist's best works. Strangers were told that Hillbridge had discovered him. The discovery had come about in the simplest manner. Professor Driffert, who had a reputation for " collecting," had one day hung a sketch on his drawing-room wall, and thereafter Mrs Driffert's visitors (always a little flurried by the sense that it was the kind of house in which one might be suddenly called upon to distinguish between a dry-point and an etching, or between Raphael Mengs and Raphael Sanzio) were not infrequently subjected to the Professor's off-hand en-

quiry, " By the way, have you seen my Keniston ?" The visitors, perceptibly awed, would retreat to a critical distance and murmur the usual guarded generalities, while they tried to keep the name in mind long enough to look it up in the Encyclopaedia. The name was not in the Encyclopaedia; but, as a compensating fact, it became known that the man himself was in Hillbridge. Hillbridge, then, owned an artist whose celebrity it was the proper thing to take for granted! Some one else, emboldened by the thought, bought a Keniston; and the next year, on the occasion of the President's golden jubilee, the Faculty, by unanimous consent, presented him with a Keniston. Two years later there was a Keniston exhibition, to which the art-critics came from New York and Boston; and not long afterward a well-known Chicago collector vainly attempted to buy Professor Driffert's sketch, which the art journals cited as a rare example of the painter's first or silvery manner. Thus there gradually grew up a small circle of connoisseurs known in artistic circles as men who collected Kenistons,

Professor Wildmarsh, of the chair of Fine Arts and Archaeology, was the first critic to publish a detailed analysis of the master's methods and purpose. The article was illustrated by engravings which (though they had cost the magazine a fortune) were declared by Professor Wildmarsh to give but an imperfect suggestion of the esoteric significance of the originals. The Professor, with a tact that contrived to make each reader feel himself included among the exceptions, went on to say that Keniston's work would never appeal to any but exceptional natures; and he closed with the usual assertion that to apprehend the full meaning of the master's " message," it was necessary to see him in the surroundings of his own home at Hillbridge.

Professor Wildmarsh's article was read one spring afternoon by a young lady just speeding eastward on her first visit to Hillbridge, and already flushed with anticipation of the intellectual opportunities awaiting her. In East Onon-daigua, where she lived, Hillbridge was looked on as an Oxford. Magazine writers, with the easy American use of the superlative, designated it as "the venerable alma mater" the "antique seat of learning," and Claudia Day had been brought up to regard it as the fountain-head of knowledge, and of that mental distinction which is so much rarer than knowledge. An innate passion for all that was thus distinguished and exceptional made her revere Hillbridge as the native soil of those intellectual amenities that were of such difficult growth in the thin air of East Onon-daigua. At the first suggestion of a visit to Hillbridge—whither she went at the invitation of a girl friend who (incredible apotheosis!) had married one of the University professors—Claudia's spirit dilated with the sense of new possibilities. The vision of herself walking under the "historic elms" toward the Memorial Library, standing rapt before the Stuart Washington, or drinking in, from some obscure corner of an academic drawing-room, the President's reminiscences of the Concord group—this vividness of self-projection into the emotions awaiting her made her glad of any delay that prolonged so exquisite a moment,

It was in this mood that she opened the article on Keniston. She knew about him, of course; she was wonderfully "well up," even for East Onondaigua. She had read of him in the magazines; she had met, on a visit to New York, a man who collected Kenistons, and a photogravure of a Keniston in an " artistic " frame hung above her writing-table at home. But Professor Wild-marsh's article made her feel how little she really knew of the master; and she trembled to think of the state of relative ignorance in which, but for the timely purchase of the magazine, she might have entered Hillbridge. She had, for instance, been densely unaware that Keniston had already had three "manners," and was showing symptoms of a fourth. She was equally ignorant of the fact that he had founded a school and " created a formula;" and she learned with a thrill that no one could hope to understand him who had not seen him in his studio at Hillbridge surrounded by his own works. " The man and the art interpret each other," their exponent declared; and Claudia Day, bend-ing a brilliant eye on the future, wondered if she were ever to be admitted to the privilege of that double initiation.

Keniston, to his other claims to distinction, added that of being hard to know. His friends always hastened to announce the fact to strangers—adding, after a pause of suspense, that they " would see what they could do." Visitors in whose favour he was induced to make an exception were further warned that he never spoke unless he was interested— so that they mustn't mind if he remained silent. It was under these reassuring conditions that, some ten days after her arrival at Hillbridge, Miss Day was introduced to the master's studio. She found him a tall listless-looking man, who appeared middle-aged to her youth, and who stood before his own pictures with a vaguely interrogative gaze, leaving the task of their interpretation to the lady who had courageously contrived the visit. The studio, to Claudia's surprise, was bare and shabby. It formed a rambling addition to the small cheerless house in which the artist lived with his mother and a widowed sister. For Claudia it added the last touch to his distinction to learn that he was poor, and that what he earned was devoted to the maintenance of the two limp women who formed a neutral - tinted background to his impressive outline. His pictures, of course, fetched high prices ; but he worked slowly —"painfully," as his devotees preferred to phrase it—with frequent intervals of ill-health and inactivity, and the circle of Keniston connoisseurs was still as small as it was distinguished. The girl's fancy instantly hailed in him that favourite figure of imaginative youth, the artist who would rather starve than paint a pot-boiler. It is known to comparatively few that the production of successful pot-boilers is an art in itself, and that such heroic abstentions as Keniston's are not always purely voluntary.

On the occasion of her first visit the artist said so little that Claudia was able to indulge to the full the harrowing sense of her inadequacy. No wonder she had not been one of the few that he cared to talk to; every word she uttered must so obviously have diminished the inducement! She had been cheap, trivial, conventional; at once gushing and inexpressive, eager and constrained. She could feel him counting the minutes till the visit was over, and as the door finally closed on the scene of her discomfiture she almost shared the hope with which she confidently credited him—that they might never meet again.

MRS DAVANT glanced reverentially about the studio. " I have always said she murmured, "that they ought to be seen in Europe."

Mrs Davant was young, credulous, and emotionally extravagant: she reminded Claudia of her earlier self—the self that, ten years before, had first set an awestruck foot on that very threshold.

"Not for his sake," Mrs Davant continued, "but for Europe's."

Claudia smiled. She was glad that her husband's pictures were to be exhibited in Paris. She concurred in Mrs Davant's view of the importance of the event; but she thought her visitor's way of putting the case a little overcharged. Ten years spent in an atmosphere of Keniston-worship had insensibly developed in Claudia a preference for moderation of speech. She believed in her husband, of course; to believe in him, with an increasing abandonment and tenacity, had become one of the necessary laws of being; but she did not believe in his admirers. Their faith in him was perhaps as genuine as her own; but it seemed to her less able to give an account of itself. Some few of his appreciators doubtless measured him by their own standards; but it was difficult not to feel that in the Hillbridge circle, where rapture ran the highest, he was accepted on what was at best but an indirect valuation; and now and then she had a frightened doubt as to the independence of her own convictions. That innate sense of relativity, which even East Onondaigua had not been able to check in Claudia Day, had been fostered in Mrs Keniston by the artistic absolutism of Hillbridge, and she often wondered that her husband remained so uncritical of the quality of admiration accorded him. Her husband's uncritical attitude toward himself and his admirers had in fact been one of the surprises of her marriage. That an artist should believe in his potential powers seemed to her at once the incentive and the pledge of excellence: she knew there was no future for a hesitating talent. What perplexed her was Keniston's satisfaction in his achievement. She had always imagined that the true artist must regard himself as the imperfect vehicle of the cosmic emotion—that beneath every difficulty overcome a new one lurked, the vision widening as the Scope enlarged. To be initiated into these creative struggles, to shed on the toiler's path the consolatory ray of faith and encouragement, had seemed the chief privilege of her marriage. But there is something supererogatory in believing in a man obviously disposed to perform that service for himself; and Claudia's ardour gradually spent itself against the dense surface of her husband's complacency. She could smile now at her vision of an intellectual communion which should admit her to the inmost precincts of his inspiration. She had learned that the creative processes are seldom self-explanatory, and Keniston's inarticulateness no longer discouraged her; but she could not reconcile her sense of the continuity of all high effort to his unperturbed air of finishing each picture as though he had despatched a masterpiece to posterity. In the first recoil from her disillusionment she even allowed herself to perceive that, if he worked slowly, it was not because he mistrusted his powers of expression, but because he had really so little to express.

" It's for Europe," Mrs Davant vaguely repeated; and Claudia noticed that she was blushingly intent on tracing with the tip of her elaborate sunshade the pattern of the shabby carpet.

" It will be a revelation to them," she went on provisionally, as though Claudia had missed her cue and left an awkward interval to fill.

Claudia had in fact a sudden sense of deficient intuition. She felt that her visitor had something to communicate which required, on her own part, an intelligent co-operation; but what it was her insight failed to suggest. She was, in truth, a little tired of Mrs Davant, who was Keniston's latest worshipper, who ordered pictures recklessly, who paid for them regally in advance, and whose gallery was, figuratively speaking, crowded with the artist's unpainted masterpieces. Claudia's impatience was perhaps complicated by the uneasy sense that Mrs Davant was too young, too rich, too inexperienced ; that somehow she ought to be warned. Warned of what? That some of the pictures might never be painted? Scarcely that, since Keniston, who was scrupulous in business transactions, might be trusted not to take any material advantage of such evidence of faith. Claudia's impulse remained undefined. She merely felt that she would have liked to help Mrs Davant, and that she did not know how.

"You'll be there to see them?" she asked, as her visitor lingered.

" In Paris ? " Mrs Davant's blush deepened. " We must all be there together."

Claudia smiled. " My husband and I mean to go abroad some day—but I don't see any chance of it at present."

" But he ought to go—you ought both to go this summer!" Mrs Davant persisted. " I know Professor \Vildmarsh and Professor Driffert and all the other o critics think that Mr Keniston's never having been to Europe has given his work much of its wonderful individuality, its peculiar flavour and meaning—but now that his talent is formed, that he has full command of his means of expression" (Claudia recognised one of Professor Driffert's favourite formulas), "they all think he ought to see the work of the other great masters—that he ought to visit the home of his ancestors, as Professor Wildmarsh says !" She stretched an impulsive hand to Claudia. " You ought to let him go, Mrs Keniston !"

Claudia accepted the admonition with the philosophy of the wife who is used to being advised on the management of her husband. " I shan't interfere with him," she declared; and Mrs Davant instantly caught her up with a cry of " Oh, it's too lovely of you to say that!" With this exclamation she left Claudia to a silent renewal of wonder.

A moment later Keniston entered: to a mind curious in combinations it might have occurred that he had met Mrs Davant on the doorstep. In one sense he might, for all his wife cared, have met fifty Mrs Davants on the doorstep: it was long since Claudia had enjoyed the solace of resenting such coincidences. Her only thought now was that her husband's first words might not improbably explain Mrs Davant's last; and she waited for him to speak.

He paused with his hands in his pockets before an unfinished picture on the easel; then, as his habit was, he began to stroll tourist-like from canvas to canvas, standing before each in a musing ecstasy of contemplation that no readjustment of view ever seemed to disturb. Her eye instinctively joined his in its inspection; it was the one point where their natures merged. Thank God, there was no doubt about the pictures! She was what she had always dreamed of being—the wife of a great artist. Keniston dropped into an armchair and filled his pipe. " How should you like to go to Europe ?" he asked.

His wife looked up quickly. " When ?"

"Now—this spring, I mean." He paused to light the pipe. " I should like to be over there while these things are being exhibited."

Claudia was silent.

" Well ? " he repeated after a moment.

" How can we afford it ? " she asked.

Keniston had always scrupulously fulfilled his duty to the mother and sister whom his marriage had dislodged; and Claudia, who had the atoning temperament which seeks to pay for every happiness by making it a source of fresh obligations, had from the outset accepted his ties with an exaggerated devotion. Any disregard of such a claim would have vulgarised her most delicate pleasures; and her husband's sensitiveness to it in great measure extenuated the artistic obtuseness that often seemed to her like a failure of the moral sense. His loyalty to the dull women who depended on him was, after all, compounded of finer tissues than any mere sensibility to ideal demands.

" Oh, I don't see why we shouldn't/' he rejoined. " I think we might manage it."

"At Mrs Davant's expense?" leaped from Claudia. She could not tell why she had said it; some inner barrier seemed to have given way under a confused pressure of emotions.

He looked up at her with frank surprise. " Well, she has been very jolly about it — why not ? She has a tremendous feeling for art—the keenest I ever knew in a woman." Claudia imperceptibly smiled. " She wants me to let her pay in advance for the four panels she has ordered for the Memorial Library. That would give us plenty of money for the trip, and my having the panels to do is another reason for my wanting to go abroad just now."

" Another reason ?"

" Yes; I've never worked on such a big scale. I want to see how those old chaps did the trick; I want to measure myself with the big fellows over there. An artist ought to, once in his life."

She gave him a wondering look. For the first time his words implied a sense of possible limitation; but his easy tone seemed to retract what they conceded. What he really wanted was fresh food for his self-satisfaction: he was like an army that moves on after exhausting the resources of the country.

Womanlike, she abandoned the general survey of the case for the consideration of a minor point.

" Are you sure you can do that kind of thing ? " she asked.

" What kind of thing ? "

"The panels."

He glanced at her indulgently: his self-confidence was too impenetrable to feel the pin-prick of such a doubt.

"Immensely sure," he said with a smile.

"And you don't mind taking so much money from her in advance?"

He stared. "Why should I? She'll get it back—with interest!" He laughed and drew at his pipe. "It will be an uncommonly interesting experience. I shouldn't wonder if it freshened me up a bit."

She looked at him again. This second hint of self-distrust struck her as the sign of a quickened sensibility. What if, after all, he was beginning to be dissatisfied with his work? The thought filled her with a renovating sense of his sufficiency.

III

THEY stopped in London to see the National Gallery.

It was thus that, in their inexperience, they had narrowly put it; but in reality every stone of the streets, every trick of the atmosphere, had its message of surprise for their virgin sensibilities. The pictures were simply the summing up, the final interpretation, of the cumulative pressure of an unimagined world; and it seemed to Claudia that long before they reached the doors of the gallery she had some intuitive revelation of what awaited them within.

They moved about from room to room without exchanging a word. The vast noiseless spaces seemed full of sound, like the roar of a distant multitude heard only by the inner ear. Had their speech been articulate their language would have been incomprehensible; and even that far-off murmur or meaning pressed intolerably on Claudia's nerves. Keniston took the onset without outward sign of disturbance. Now and then he paused before a canvas, or prolonged from one of the benches his silent communion with some miracle of line or colour; but he neither looked at his wife nor spoke to her. He seemed to have forgotten her presence.

Claudia was conscious of keeping a furtive watch on him; but the sum total of her impressions was negative. She

remembered thinking when she first met him that his face was rather expressionless; and he had the habit of self-engrossed silences.

All that evening, at the hotel, they talked about London, and he surprised her by an acuteness of observation that she had sometimes inwardly accused him of lacking. He seemed to have seen everything, to have examined, felt, compared, with nerves as finely adjusted as her own; but he said nothing of the pictures. The next day they returned to the National Gallery, and he began to study the paintings in detail, pointing out differences of technique, analyzing and criticising, but still without summing up his conclusions. He seemed to have a sort of provincial dread of showing himself too much impressed. Claudia's own sensations were too complex, too overwhelming, to be readily classified. Lacking the craftsman's instinct to steady her, she felt herself carried off her feet by the rush of incoherent impressions. One point she consciously avoided, and that was the comparison of her husband's work with what they were daily seeing.

Art, she inwardly argued, was too various, too complex, dependent on too many inter-relations of feeling and environment, to allow of its being judged by any provisional standard. Even the subtleties of technique must be modified by the artist's changing purpose, as this in turn is acted on by influences of which he is himself unconscious. How, then, was an unprepared imagination to distinguish between such varied reflections of the elusive vision? She took refuge in a passionate exaggeration of her own ignorance and insufficiency.

After a week in London they went to Paris. The exhibition of Keniston's pictures had been opened a few days earlier; and as they drove through the streets on the way to the station an "impressionist" poster here and there invited them to the display of the American artist's work. Mrs Davant, who had been in Paris for the opening, had already written rapturously of the impression produced, enclosing commendatory notices from one or two papers. She reported that there had been a great crowd on the first day, and that the critics had been "immensely struck."

The Kenistons arrived in the evening, and the next morning Claudia, as a matter of course, asked her husband at what time he meant to go and see the pictures.

He looked up absently from his guidebook.

"What pictures?"

"Why—yours," she said, surprised.

"Oh, they'll keep," he answered; adding with a slightly embarrassed laugh, "We'll give the other chaps a show first." Presently he laid down his book and proposed that they should go to the Louvre.

They spent the morning there, lunched at a restaurant near by, and returned to the gallery in the afternoon. Keniston had passed from inarticulateness to an eager volubility. It was clear that he was beginning to co-ordinate his impressions, to find his way about in a corner of the great imaginative universe. He seemed extraordinarily ready to impart his discoveries; and Claudia felt that her ignorance served him as a convenient buffer against the terrific impact of new sensations.

On the way home she asked when he meant to see Mrs Davant.

His answer surprised her. "Does she know we're here?"

"Not unless you've sent her word," said Claudia, with a touch of harmless irony.

"That's all right, then," he returned simply. "I want to wait and look about a day or two longer. She'd want us to go sight-seeing with her; and I'd rather get my impressions alone."

The next two days were hampered by the necessity of eluding Mrs Davant. Claudia, under different circumstances, would have scrupled to share in this somewhat shabby conspiracy; but she found herself in a state of suspended judgment, wherein her husband's treatment of Mrs Davant became for the moment merely a clue to larger meanings.

They had been four days in Paris when Claudia, returning one afternoon from a parenthetical excursion to the Rue de la Paix, was confronted on her threshold by the reproachful figure of their benefactress. It was not to her, however, that Mrs Davant's reproaches were addressed. Keniston, it appeared, had borne the brunt of them; for he stood leaning against the mantelpiece of their modest salon in that attitude of convicted negligence when, if ever, a man is glad to take refuge behind his wife.

Claudia had however no immediate intention of affording him such shelter. She wanted to observe and wait.

"He's too impossible!" cried Mrs Davant, sweeping her at once into the central current of her grievance.

Claudia looked from one to the other.

"For not going to see you?"

" For not going to see his pictures!" cried the other nobly.

Claudia coloured and Keniston shifted his position uneasily.

" I can't make her understand," he said, turning to his wife.

"I don't care about myself!" Mrs Davant interjected.

" do, then; it's the only thing I do care about," he hurriedly protested. " I meant to go at once—to write—Claudia wanted to go, but I wouldn't let her,"

He looked helplessly about the pleasant red-curtained room, which was rapidly burning itself into Claudia's consciousness as a visible extension of Mrs Davant's claims.

" I can't explain," he broke off.

Mrs Davant in turn addressed herself to Claudia.

"People think it's so odd," she complained. " So many of the artists here are anxious to meet him ; they've all been so charming about the pictures; and several of our American friends have come over from London expressly for the exhibition. I told every one that he would be here for the opening—there was a private view, you know—and they were so disappointed—they wanted to give him an ovation; and 1 didn't know what to say. What am I to say ?" she abruptly ended.

" There's nothing to say," said Keniston slowly.

" But the exhibition closes the day after to-morrow."

" Well, shan't close—I shall be here," he declared, with an effort at playfulness. " If they want to see me—all these people

you're kind enough to mention—won't there be other chances ?"

" But I wanted them to see you among your pictures—to hear you talk about them, explain them in that wonderful way. I wanted you to interpret each other, as Professor Wildmarsh says ! "

" Oh, hang Professor Wildmarsh !" said Keniston, softening the commination with a smile. "If my pictures are good for anything they oughtn't to need explaining."

Mrs Davant stared. "But I thought that was what made them so interesting!" she exclaimed.

Keniston looked down. " Perhaps it was," he murmured.

There was an awkward silence, which Claudia broke by saying, with a glance at her husband: " But if the exhibition is to remain open to-morrow, could we not meet you there ? And perhaps you could send word to some of our friends."

Mrs Davant brightened like a child whose broken toy is glued together. " Oh, do make him !" she implored. " I'll ask them to come in the afternoon—we'll make it into a little tea — a jive o'clock.

['11 send word at once to everybody!" She gathered up her beruffled boa and sunshade, settling her plumage like a reassured bird. " It will be too lovely !" she ended in a self-consoling murmur.

But in the doorway a new doubt assailed her. "You won't fail me?" she said, turning plaintively to Keniston. " You'll make him come, Mrs Keniston ?"

" I'll bring him !" Claudia promised.

IV

WHEN, the next morning, she appeared equipped for their customary ramble, her husband surprised her by announcing that he meant to stay at home.

" The fact is, I'm rather surfeited," he said, smiling. " I suppose my appetite isn't equal to such a plethora. 1 think I'll write some letters and join you somewhere later."

She detected the wish to be alone, and responded to it with her usual readiness.

" I shall sink to my proper level and buy a bonnet, then," she said. " I haven't had time to take the edge off that appetite."

They agreed to meet at the Hotel Cluny at mid-day, and she set out alone with a vague sense of relief. Neither she nor Keniston had made any direct reference to Mrs Davant's visit; but its effect was implicit in their eagerness to avoid each other.

Claudia accomplished some shopping in the spirit of perfunctoriness that robs even new bonnets of their bloom; and this business despatched, she turned aimlessly into the wide inviting brightness of the streets. Never had she felt more isolated amid that ordered beauty which gives a social quality to the very stones and mortar of Paris. All about her were evidences of an artistic sensibility pervading every form of life like the nervous structure of the huge frame—a sensibility so delicate, alert, and universal, that it seemed to leave no room for obtuseness or error. In such a medium the faculty of plastic expression must develop as unconsciously as any organ in its normal surroundings ; to be " artistic" must cease to be an attitude and become a natural function. To Claudia the significance of the whole vast revelation was centred in the light it

shed on one tiny spot of consciousness— the value of her husband's work. There are moments when, to the groping soul, the world's accumulated experiences are but stepping-stones across a private difficulty.

She stood hesitating at a street corner. It was barely eleven, and she had an hour to spare before going to the Hotel Cluny. She seemed to be letting her inclination float as it would on the cross-currents of suggestion emanating from the brilliant complex scene before her; but suddenly, in obedience to an impulse that she became aware of only in acting on it, she called a cab and drove to the gallery where her husband's pictures were exhibited.

A magnificent official in gold braid sold her a ticket, and pointed the way up the empty crimson - carpeted stairs. His duplicate, on the upper landing, held out a catalogue with an air of recognizing the futility of the offer; and a moment later she found herself in the long, noiseless impressive room, full of velvet-covered ottomans and exotic plants. It was clear that the public ardour on which Mrs H

Davant had expatiated had spent itseli earlier in the week; for Claudia had this luxurious apartment to herself. Something about its air of rich privacy, its diffusion of that sympathetic quality in other countries so conspicuously absent from the public showroom, seemed to emphasize its present emptiness. It was as though the flowers, the carpet, the lounges, surrounded their visitor's solitary advance with the mute assurance that they had done all they could toward making the thing "go off," and that if they had failed it was simply for lack of co-operation. She stood still and looked about her. The pictures struck her instantly as odd gaps in the general harmony; it was self-evident that they had not co-operated. They had not been pushing, aggressive, discordant: they had merely effaced themselves. She swept a startled eye from one familiar painting to another. The canvases were all there —and the frames—but the miracle, the mirage of life and meaning, had vanished like some atmospheric illusion. What was it that had happened? And had it happened to her or to the pictures ? She

tried to rally her frightened thoughts; to push or coax them into semblance of resistance;

but argument was swept off its feet by the huge rush of a single conviction — the conviction that the pictures were bad. There was no standing up against that : she felt herself submerged.

The stealthy fear that may have been following her all these days had her by the throat now. The great vision of beauty through which she had been moving, as one enchanted, was turned to a phantasmagoria of evil-mocking shapes. She hated the past; she hated its splendour, its power, its wicked magical vitality. . . She dropped into a seat and continued to stare at the. wall before her. Gradually, as she stared, there stole out to her from the dimmed humbled canvases a reminder of what she had once seen in them, a spectral appeal to her faith to call them back to life. What proof had she that the present estimate of them was less subjective than the other? The confused impressions of the last few days were hardly to be pleaded as a valid theoiy of art. How, after all, did she know that the pictures were bad ? On what suddenly acquired technical standard had she thus decided the case against them? It seemed as though it were a standard outside of herself, as though some unheeded inner sense were gradually making her aware of the presence, in that empty room, of a critical intelligence that was giving out a subtle effluence of disapproval. The fancy was so vivid that, to shake it off, she rose and began to move about again. In the middle of the room stood a monumental divan surmounted by a massif of palms and azaleas. As Claudia's muffled wanderings carried her round the angle of this seat, she saw that its further side was occupied by the figure of a man, who sat with his hands resting on his stick and his head bowed upon them. She gave a little cry, and her husband rose and faced her.

Instantly the live point of consciousness was shifted, and she became aware that the quality of the pictures no longer mattered. It was what he thought of them that counted: her life hung on that.

They looked at each other a moment in silence; such concussions are not apt to flash into immediate speech. At length he said simply, " I didn't know you were coming here."

She coloured as though he had charged her with something underhand.

" I didn't mean to," she stammered; "but I was too early for our appointment "

Her words cast a revealing glare on the situation. Neither of them looked at the pictures; but to Claudia those unobtruding presences seemed suddenly to press upon them and force them apart.

Keniston glanced at his watch. " It's twelve o'clock," he said, "shall we go on?"

AT the door he called a cab and put her in it; then, drawing out his watch again, he said abruptly: " I believe I'll let you go alone. I'll join you at the hotel in time for luncheon." She wondered for a moment if he meant to return to the

gallery; but, looking back as she drove off, she saw him walk rapidly away in the opposite direction.

The cabman had carried her half-way to the Hotel Cluny before she realized where she was going, and cried out to him to turn home. There was an acute irony in this mechanical prolongation of the quest of beauty. She had had enough of it, too much of it; her one longing was to escape, to hide herself away from its all-suffusing implacable light.

At the hotel, alone in her room, a few tears came to soften her seared vision ; but her mood was too tense to be eased by weeping. Her whole being was centred in the longing to know what her husband thought. Their short exchange of words had, after all, told her nothing. She had guessed a faint resentment at her unexpected appearance; but that might merely imply a dawning sense, on his part, of being furtively watched and criticised. She had sometimes wondered if he was never conscious of her observation ; there were moments when it seemed to radiate from her in visible waves.

Perhaps, after all, he was aware of it, on his guard against it, as a lurking knife behind the thick curtain of his complacency ; and to-day he must have caught the gleam of the blade.

Claudia had not reached the age when pity is the first chord to vibrate in contact with any revelation of failure. Her one hope had been that Keniston should be clear-eyed enough to face the truth. Whatever it turned out to be, she wanted him to measure himself with it. But as his image rose before her she felt a sudden half-maternal longing to thrust herself between him and disaster. Her eagerness to see him tested by circumstances seemed now like a cruel scientific curiosity. She saw in a flash of sympathy that he would need her most if he fell beneath his fate.

He did not, after all, return for luncheon; and when she came upstairs from her solitary meal their salon was still untenanted. She permitted herself no sensational fears; for she could not, at the height of apprehension, figure Keniston as yielding to any tragic impulse ; but the lengthening hours brought

an uneasiness that was fuel to her pity. Suddenly she heard the clock strike five. It was the hour at which they had promised to meet Mrs Davant at the gallery — the hour of the " ovation." Claudia rose and went to the window, straining for a glimpse of her husband in the crowded street. Could it be that he had forgotten her, had gone to the gallery without her ? Or had something happened — that veiled " something " which, for the last hour, had grimly hovered on the outskirts of her mind ?

She heard a hand on the door and Keniston entered. As she turned to meet him her whole being was swept forward on a great wave of pity: she was so sure, now, that he must know.

But he confronted her with a glance of preoccupied brightness; her first impression was that she had never seen him so vividly, so expressively pleased. If he needed her it was not to bind up his wounds.

He gave her a smile which was clearly the lingering reflection of some inner light. "1 didn't mean to be so late," he said, tossing aside his hat and the

little red volume that served as a clue to his explorations. " I turned in to the Louvre for a minute after I left you this morning, and the place fairly swallowed me up—I couldn't get away from it. I've been there ever since." He threw himself into a chair and glanced about for his pipe.

" It takes time," he continued musingly, " to get at them, to make out what they're saying—the big fellows, 1 mean. They're not a communicative lot. At first I couldn't make much out of their lingo—it was too different from mine! But gradually, by picking up a hint here and there, and piecing them together, I've begun to understand; and to-day, by Jove, I got one or two of the old chaps by the throat and fairly turned them inside out—made them deliver up their last drop." He lifted a brilliant eye to her. " Lord, it was tremendous !" he declared.

He had found his pipe and was musingly rilling it. Claudia waited in silence.

" At first," he began again, " I was at raid their language was too hard for

me—that I should never quite know what they were driving at; they seemed to cold-shoulder me, to be bent on shutting me out. But I was bound I wouldn't be beaten, and now, to-day—" he paused a moment to strike a match—"when I went to look at those things of mine it all came over me in a flash. By Jove ! it was as if I'd made them all into a big bonfire to light me on my road!"

His wife was trembling with a kind of sacred terror. She had been afraid to pray for light for him, and he was joyfully casting his whole past upon the pyre!

" Is there nothing left ?" she faltered. " Nothing left ? There's everything !" he exulted. "Why, here I am, not much over forty, and I've found out already—already!" He stood up and began to move excitedly about the room. " My God ! Suppose I'd never known ! Suppose I'd gone on painting things like that for ever! Why, I feel like those chaps at revivalist meetings when they get up and say they're saved! Won't somebody please start a hymn ?" Claudia, with a tremulous joy was

THE RECOVERY

letting herself go on the strong current of his emotion; but it had not yet carried her beyond her depth, and suddenly she felt hard ground underfoot.

Mrs Davant " she exclaimed.

"He stared, as though suddenly recalled from a long distance. " Mrs Davant ?"

" We were to have met her—this afternoon—now "

" At the gallery ? Oh, that's all right. I put a stop to that; I went to see her after I left you ; I explained it all to her."

"All?"

" I told her I was going to begin all over again."

Claudia's heart gave a forward bound and then sank back hopelessly.

" But the panels ?"

" That's all right too. I told her about the panels," he reassured her.

"You told her ?"

" That I can't paint them now. She doesn't understand, of course; but she's the best little woman, and she trusts me."

She could have wept for joy at his exquisite obtuseness. "But that isn't all," she wailed. " It doesn't matter how much you've explained to her. It doesn't do away with the fact that we're living on those panels!"

" Living on them ?"

"On the money that she paid you to paint them. Isn't that what brought us here ? And—if you mean to do as you say—to begin all over again—how in the world are we ever to pay her back ?"

Her husband turned on her an inspired eye. " There's only one way that I know of," he imperturbably declared, " and that's to stay out here till I learn how to paint them."

"COPY"

IV "COPY"

A DIALOGUE

AMBROSE DALE— forty, slender, still young — sits in her drawing-room at the tea table. The winter twilight is falling, a lamp has been lit, there is a fire on the hearth, and the room is pleasantly dim and flmver- scented. Books are scattered everywhere — mostly with autograph inscriptions "From the Author" — and a large portrait of Mrs Dale, at her desk, with papers strewn about her, takes up one of the wall-panels. Before Mrs Dale stands Hilda, fair and twenty, her hands full of letters.

DALE. — Ten more applications for autographs ? Isn't it strange that people who'd blush to borrow twenty dollars don't scruple to beg for an autograph ?

Hilda (reproachfully). —Oh—

Mrs Dale. —What's the difference, pray?

Hilda. —Only that your last autograph sold for fifty-

Mrs Dale (not displeased). —Ah ?—I sent for you, Hilda, because I'm dining out to-night, and if there's nothing important to attend to among these letters you needn't sit up for me.

Hilda. —You don't mean to work ?

Mrs Dale. —Perhaps; but I shan't need you. You'll see that my cigarettes and coffee-machine are in place, and that I don't have to crawl about the floor in search of my pen-wiper? That's all. Now about these letters

Hilda (impulsively). —Oh, Mrs Dale

Mrs Dale.—Well ?

Hilda. —I'd rather sit up for you.

Mrs Dale. —Child, I've nothing for you to do. I shall be blocking out the tenth chapter of Winged Purposes, and it won't be ready for you till next week.

Hilda. —It isn't that; but it's so beautiful to sit here, watching and listening, all alone in the night, and to feel that you're in there (she points to the study-door) creating— - (Impulsively.) What do I care for sleep ?

Mrs Dale (indulgently). —Child—silly child!—Yes, I should have felt so at your age—it would have been an inspiration

Hilda (rapt). —It is!

Mrs Dale. —But you must go to bed; I must have you fresh in the morning; for you're still at the age when one is fresh in the morning! (She sighs.) The letters? (Abruptly.) Do you take notes of what you feel, Hilda—here, all alone in the night, as you say ?

Hilda (shyly). —I have

Mrs Dale (smiling). —For the diaiy ?

Hilda nods and blushes.

Mrs Dale (caressingly). —Goose!—Well, to business. What is there ?

Hilda. —Nothing important, except a letter from Stroud & Fayerweather to say that the question of the royalty on Pomegranate Seed has been settled in your favour. The English publishers of Immolation write to consult you about a six-shilling edition; Olafson, the Copen-i hagen publisher, applies for permission to bring out a Danish translation of The Idol's Feet; and the editor of the Semaphore wants a new serial—I think that's all; except that Woman s Sphere and The Droplight ask for interviews—with photographs

Mrs Dale. —The same old story! I'm so tired of it all. (To herself, in an undertone.\'7d But how should I feel if it all stopped ? (The servant brings in a card.\'7d

Mrs Dale (reading it). —Is it possible ? Paul Ventnor? (To the servant.) Show Mr Ventnor up. (To herself.) Paul Ventnor!

Hilda (breathless). —Oh, Mrs Dale— the Mr Ventnor ?

Mrs Dale (smiling). —I fancy there's only one.

Hilda. —The great, great poet? (Irresolute.) No, 1 don't dare

Mrs Dale (with a tinge of impatience\'7d. -What?

Hilda (fervently). — Ask you — if I might—oh, here in this corner, where he can't possibly notice me—stay just a moment? Just to see him come in? To see the meeting between you — the

greatest novelist and the greatest poet of the age ? Oh, it's too much to ask! It's an historic moment.

(Why, I suppose it is. I hadn't thought of it in that light. Well (smiling), for the diary—

Hilda. —Oh, thank you, thank you I'll be off the very instant I've heard him speak.

Mrs Dale. —The very instant, mind. (She rises, looks at *herself* in the glass, smooths her hair, sits down again, and rattles the tea-caddy.) Isn't the room very warm ? — (She looks over at her portrait.) I've grown stouter since that was painted - - You'll make a fortune out of that diary, Hilda

Hilda (modestly). — Four publishers have applied to me already—

The Servant announces. — Mr Paul Ventnor.

(Tall, nearing fifty, with an incipient stoutness buttoned into a masterly frock-coat, Ventnor drops his glass and advances vaguely, with a short-sighted stare.)

Ventnor. —Mrs Dale ?

Mrs Dale. — My dear friend! This is kind. (She looks over her shoulder at Hilda, who vanishes through the door to the left.) The papers announced your arrival, but I hardly hoped

Ventnor (whose short-sighted stare is seen to conceal a deeper embarrassment). —You hadn't forgotten me, then ?

Mrs Dale. —Delicious ! Do you forget that you're public property ?

Ventnor. —Forgotten, I mean, that we were old friends?

Mrs Dale. —Such old friends! May I remind you that it's nearly twenty years since we've met? Or do you find cold reminiscences indigestible ?

Ventnor. —On the contrary, I've come to ask you for a dish of them—we'll warm them up together. You're my first visit.

Mrs Dale. —How perfect of you ! So few men visit their women friends in chronological order; or at least they generally do it the other way round, beginning with the present day and working back—if there's time—to prehistoric woman.

Ventnor. —But when prehistoric woman has become historic woman ?

Mrs Dale. —Oh, it's the reflection of my glory that has guided you here, then?

Vuitnor. —It's a spirit in my feet that has led me, at the first opportunity, to the most delightful spot I know.

Mrs Dale. —Oh, the first opportunity !

Ventnor. —I might have seen you very often before ; but never just in the right way.

Mrs Dale. —Is this the right way ?

Ventnor. —It depends on you to make it so.

Mrs Dale. — What a responsibility ! What shall I do ?

Ventnor. —Talk to me—make me think you're a little glad to see me; give me some tea and a cigarette; and say you're out to every one else.

Mrs Dale.—Is that all? (She hands him a cup of tea.) The cigarettes are at your elbow And do you think I shouldn't have been glad to see you before ?

Ventnor. —No; I think I should have been too glad to see you.

Mrs Dale. —Dear me, what precautions ! I hope you always wear goloshes when it looks like rain and never by any chance expose yourself to a draught. But I had an idea that poets courted the emotions—

Ventnor. —Do novelists ?

Mrs Dale. —If you ask me —on paper!

Ventnor. —Just so; that's safest. My best things about the sea have been written on shore. (He looks at her thoughtfully.) But it wouldn't have suited us in the old days, would it?

Mrs Dale (sighing). —When we were real people!

Ventnor. —Real people?

Mrs Dale. —Are you, now? I died years ago. What you see before you is a figment of the reporter's brain—a monster manufactured out of newspaper paragraphs, with ink in its veins. A keen sense of copyright is my nearest approach to an emotion.

Ventnor (sighing\'7d. —Ah, well, yes—as you say, we're public property.

Mrs Dale. —If one shared equally with the public! But the last shred of my identity is gone.

Ventnor. —Most people would be glad to part with them on such terms. I have followed your work with immense interest. Immolation is a masterpiece. I read it last summer when it first came out.

Mrs Dale (with a shade less warmth). — Immolation has been out three years.

Ventnor. —Oh, by Jove—no? Surely not But one is so overwhelmed—one loses count. (Reproachfully.) Why have you never sent me your books?

Mrs Dale. —For that very reason.

Ventnor (deprecatingly\'7d. —You know I didn't mean it for you! And my first book—do you remember—was dedicated to you.

Mrs Dale. — Silver Trumpets

Ventnor (much interested\'7d. —Have you a copy still, by any chance? The first edition, I mean? Mine was stolen years ago. Do you think you could put your hand on it?

Mrs Dale (taking a small shabby book from the table at her side\'7d. —It's here.

Ventnor (eagerly\'7d. —May I have it? Ah, thanks. This is very interesting. The last copy sold in London for £40, and they tell me the next will fetch twice as much. It's quite introuvable.

Mrs Dale. — I know that. (A pause.

She takes the book from him, opens it, and reads, half to herself—)

" How much we two have seen together,

Of other eyes unwist, Dear as in days of leafless weather The willow's saffron mist,

Strange as the hour when Hesper swings

A-sea in heryl green, "While overhead on dalliant wings

The daylight hangs serene,

And thrilling as a meteor's fall

Through depths of lonely sky, "When each to each two watchers call:

I saw it!—So did I."

Ventnor. —Thin, thin—the troubadour tinkle. Odd how little promise there is in first volumes!

Mrs Dale (with irresistible emphasis). — I thought there was a distinct promise in this!

Ventnor (seeing his mistake). —Ah—the one you would never let me fulfil? (Sentimentally.) How inexorable you were! You never dedicated a book to me.

Mrs Dale. —I hadn't begun to write when we were—dedicating things to each other.

Ventnor. —Not for the public—but you wrote for me; and, wonderful as you are, you've never written anything since that I care for half as much as

Mrs Dale (interested). —Well?

Ventnor. —Your letters.

Mrs Dale (in a changed voice). — My letters—do you remember them ?

Ventnor. —When I don't, I re-read them,

Mrs Dale (incredulous). —You have them still ?

Ventnor (unguardedly). —You haven't mine, then ?

Mrs Dale (playfully). —Oh, you were a celebrity already. Of course I kept them ! (Smiling.) Think what they are worth now! I always keep them locked up in my safe over there. (She indicates a cabinet.)

Ventnor (after a pause). —I always carry yours with me.

Mrs Dale (laughing). —You

Ventnor. —Wherever I go. (A longer pause. She looks at him fixedly.\'7d I have them with me now.

Mrs Dale (agitated). —You—have them with you—now ?

Ventnor (embarrassed). — Why not? One never knows

Mrs Dale. —Never knows ?

Ventnor (humorously). —Gad—when the bank-examiner may come round. You forget I'm a married man.

Mrs Dale. —Ah—yes.

Ventnor (sits down beside her). —I speak to you as I couldn't to anyone else—without deserving a kicking. You know how it all came about. (A pause.) You'll bear witness that it wasn't till you denied me all hope

Mrs Dale (a little breathless). —Yes, yes

Ventnor. —Till you sent me from you

Mrs Dale. —It's so easy to be heroic when one is young! One doesn't realize how long life is going to last afterward. (Musing.) Nor what weary work it is gathering up the fragments.

Ventnor. —But the time comes when one sends for the china-mender, and has the bits riveted together, and turns the cracked side to the wall

Mrs Dale. —And denies that the article was ever damaged ?

Ventnor. — Eh ? Well, the great thing, you see, is to keep one's self out of reach of the housemaid's brush. (A pause.) If you're married you can't — always. (Smiling.) Don't you hate to be taken down and dusted ?

Mrs Dale (with intention). — You forget how long ago my husband died. It's fifteen years since I've been an object of interest to anybody but the public.

Ventnor (smiling). — The only one of your admirers to whom you've ever given the least encouragement!

Mrs Dale. —Say rather the most easily pleased!

Ventnor. — Or the only one you cared to please ?

Mrs Dale. — Ah, you haven t kept my letters !

Ventnor (gravely). — Is that a challenge ? Look here, then ! (He draws a packet from his pocket and holds it out to her.)

Mrs Dale (taking the packet and looking at him earnestly). —Why have you brought me these ?

Ventnor. — I didn't bring them; they came because I came— that's all. (Tentatively.) Are we unwelcome ?

Mrs Dale (who has undone the packet and does not appear to hear him). —The very first I ever wrote you—the day after we met at the concert. How on earth did you happen to keep it ? (SJie glances over it.) How perfectly absurd ! Well, it's not a compromising document.

Ventnor. —I'm afraid none of them are.

Mrs Dale (quickly). —Is it to that they owe their immunity ? Because one could leave them about like safety matches ? — Ah, here's another I remember—I wrote that the day after we went skating together for the first time. (She reads it slowly.) How odd ! How very odd!

Ventnor.— What?

Mrs Dale. — Why, it's the most curious thing—I had a letter of this kind to do the other day, in the novel I'm at work on now—the letter of a woman who is just—just beginning

Ventnor. —Yes—just beginning ?

Mrs Dale. —And, do you know, I find the best phrase in it, the phrase I somehow regarded as the fruit of — well, of all my subsequent discoveries — is simply plagiarized, word for word, from this!

Ventnor (eagerly). —I told you so! You were all there !

Mrs Dale (critically). —But the rest of it's poorly done—very poorly. (Reads the letter over.) —H'm—I didn't know how to leave off. It takes me for ever to get out of the door.

Ventnor (gaily). —Perhaps I was there to prevent you! (After a pause.) I wonder what I said in return ?

Mrs Dale (interested). —Shall we look? (She rises.\'7d Shall we—really? I have them all here, you know. (She goes toward the cabinet.)

Ventnor (following her with repressed eagerness). —Oh— all!

Mrs Dale (throws open the door of the cabinet, revealing a number of packets). — Don't you believe me now ?

Ventnor. —Good heavens ! How I must have repeated myself! But then you were so very deaf.

Mrs Dale (takes out a packet and returns to her seat. Ventnor extends an impatient hand for the letters). —No—no; wait! I want to find your answer to the one I was just reading. (After a pause.\'7d Here it is—yes, I thought so!

Ventnor. — What did you think ?

Mrs Dale (triumphantly). —I thought it was the one in which you quoted Epipsychidion

Ventnor. —Mercy ! Did I quote things ? I don't wonder you were cruel.

Mrs Dale. —Ah, and here's the other— the one I —the one I didn't answer—for a long time. Do you remember ?

Ventnor (with emotion\'7d. —Do I remember? I wrote it the morning after we heard Isolde

Mrs Dale (disappointed). —No - - no. That wasn't the one I didn't answer! Here—this is the one I mean.

Ventnor (takes it curiously\'7d. —Ah—h'm —this is very like unrolling a mummy— (he glances at her\'7d —with a live grain of wheat in it, perhaps ?—Oh, by Jove !

Mrs Dale.— What ?

Ventnor. —Why, this is the one I made a sonnet out of afterward ! By Jove, I'd forgotten where that idea came from. You may know the lines perhaps? They're in the fourth volume of my Complete Edition —It's the thing beginning,

" Love came to me with unrelenting eyes "—

one of my best, I rather fancy. Of course, here it's very crudely put— the values aren't brought out—ah ! this touch is good though— very good. H'm, I daresay there might be other material. (He glances toward the cabinet.)

Mrs Dale (drily).—The live grain of wheat, as you said !

Ventnor. — Ah, well—my first harvest was sown on rocky ground — now I plant for the fowls of the air. (Rising and walking toward the, cabinet.) When can I come and carry off all this rubbish ?

Mrs Dale. —Carry it off?

Ventnor (embarrassed). — My dear lady, surely between you and me explicitness is a burden. You must see that these letters of ours can't be left to take their chance like an ordinary correspondence— you said yourself we were public property.

Mrs Dale. — To take their chance ? Do you suppose that, in my keeping, your letters take any chances? (Suddenly.) Do mine—in yours ?

Ventnor (still more embarrassed). — Helen— —! (He takes a turn through the room.) You force me to remind you that you and I are differently situated—

that in a moment of madness I sacrificed the only right you ever gave me — the right to love you better than any other woman in the world. (A pause. She says nothing, and he continues, with increasing

difficulty) You asked me just now

why I carried your letters about with me — kept them, literally, in my own hands. Well, suppose it's to be sure of their not falling into some one else's ?

Mrs Dale.—Oh !

Ventnor (throws himself into a chair). — For God's sake, don't pity me !

Mrs Dale (after a long pause). — Am I dull—or are you trying to say that you want to give me back my letters ?

Ventnor (starting up). — I ? Give you back ? God forbid! Your letters? Not for the world! The only thing I have left! But you can't dream that in my hands

Mrs Dale (suddenly). — You want yours, then?

Ventnor (repressing his eagerness). — My dear friend, if I'd ever dreamed that you'd kept them ?

Mrs Dale (accusingly). — You do want them. (A pause. He makes a depre-calory gesture.) Why should they be less safe with me than mine with you ? I never forfeited the right to keep them.

Ventnor (after another pause). —It's compensation enough, almost, to have you reproach me! (He moves nearer to her, but she makes no response.) You forget that I've forfeited all my rights-even that of letting you keep my letters.

Mrs Dale. —You do want them ! (She rises, throws all the letters into the cabinet, locks the door and puts the key in her pocket.) There's my answer.

Ventnor. —Helen— —!

Mrs Dale. —Ah, I paid dearly enough for the right to keep them, and I mean to ! (She turns to him passionately.) Have you ever asked yourself how I paid for it? With what months and years of solitude, what indifference to flattery, what resistance to affection?—Oh, don't smile because I said affection, and not love. Affection's a warm cloak in cold weather; and I have been cold; and I shall keep on growing colder! Don't talk to me about living in the hearts of my readers! We both know what kind of a domicile that is. Why, before long I shall become a classic! Bound in sets and kept on the top book-shelf— brr, doesn't that sound freezing? I foresee the day when I shall be as lonely as an Etruscan museum! (She breaks into a laugh.) That's what I've paid for the right to keep your letters. (She holds out her hand.) And now give me mine.

Ventnor. —Yours ?

Mrs Dale (haughtily). —Yes ; I claim them.

Ventnor (in the same tone). — On what ground ?

Mrs Dale. —Hear the man!—Because 1 wrote them, of course.

Ventnor. —But it seems to me that— under your inspiration, I admit—I also wrote mine.

Mrs Dale. —Oh, I don't dispute their authenticity—it's yours I deny!

Ventnor. —Mine ?

Mrs Dale. —You voluntarily ceased to be the man who wrote me those letters— you've admitted as much. You traded paper for flesh and blood. I don't dispute your wisdom—only you must hold to your bargain! The letters are all mine.

Ventnor (groping between two tones). — Your arguments are as convincing as ever. (He hazard* a faint laugh.) You're a marvellous dialectician—but, if we're going to settle the matter in the spirit of an arbitration treaty, why, there are accepted conventions in such cases. It's an odious way to put it, but since you won't help me, one of them is

Mrs Dale. —One of them is ?

Ventnor. —That it is usual—that technically, I mean, the letter— belongs to its writer

Mrs Dale (after a pause). —Such letters as these ?

Ventnor. —Such letters especially

Mrs Dale. — But you couldn't have written them if I hadn't — been willing to read them. Surely there's more of myself in them than of you.

Ventnor. —Surely there's nothing in which a man puts more of himself than in his love-letters !

Mrs Dale (with emotion). — But a woman's love-letters are like her child. They belong to her more than to anybody else

Ventnor. — And a man's ?

Mrs Dale (with sudden violence). — Are all he risks!—There, take them. (She flings the key of the cabinet at his feet and sinks into a chair.)

Ventnor (starts as though to pick up the key; then approaches and bends over her).— Helen—Oh, Helen !

Mrs Dale (she yields her hands to him, murmuring:)— Paul! (Suddenly she straightens herself and draws back illuminated.) What a fool I am! I see it all now. You want them for your memoirs!

Ventnor (disconcerted). —Helen

Mrs Dale (agitated). —Come, come— the rule is to unmask when the signal's given 1 You want them for your memoirs.

Ventnor (with a forced laugh). —What makes you think so?

Mrs Dale (triumphantly). —Because want them for mine!

Ventnor (in a changed tone). —Ah !— (He moves away from her and leans against the mantelpiece. She remains seated, with her eyes fixed on him.)

Mrs Dale. —I wonder I didn't see it sooner. Your reasons were lame enough.

"COPY"

Ventnor (ironically). — Yours were masterly. You're the most accomplished actor of the two. I was completely deceived.

Mrs Dale. — Oh, I'm a novelist. I can keep up that sort of thing for five hundred pages !

Ventnor. —I congratulate you. (A pause.)

Mrs Dale (moving to her seat behind the tea-table). — I've never offered you any tea. (She bends over the kettle.) Why don't you take your letters?

Ventnor. —Because you've been clever enough to make it impossible for me. (He picks up the key and hands it to her. Then abruptly.) — Was it all acting—just now?

Mrs Dale. —By what right do you ask?

Ventnor. — By right of renouncing my claim to my letters. Keep them—and tell me.

Mrs Dale. — I give you back your claim—and I refuse to tell you.

Ventnor (sadly). — Ah, Helen, if you deceived me, you deceived yourself also.

that we're both undeceived ? I played a losing game, that's all.

Ventnor. — Why losing — since all the letters are yours?

Mrs Dale.— The letters? (Slowly.) I'd forgotten the letters

Ventnor (exultant). — Ah, I knew you'd end by telling me the truth!

Mrs Dale.— The truth ? Where is the truth? (Half to herself.) I thought I was lying when I began— but the lies turned into truth as I uttered them! (She looks at Ventnor.) I did want your letters for my memoirs— I did think I'd kept them for that purpose—and I wanted to get mine back for the same reason—but now (she puts out her hand and picks up some of her letters, which are lying scattered on the table near her) — how fresh they seem, and how they take me back to the time when we lived instead of writing about life!

Ventnor (smiling). — The time when we didn't prepare our impromptu effects beforehand and copyright our remarks about the weather!

Mrs Dale. — Or keep our epigrams in
cold storage and our adjectives under lock and keyl

Ventnor. —When our emotions weren't worth ten cents a word, and a signature wasn't an autograph. Ah, Helen, after all, there's nothing like the exhilaration of spending one's capital!

Mrs Dale. —Of wasting it, you mean. (She points to the letters.) Do you suppose we could have written a word of these if we'd known we were putting our dreams out at interest ? (She sits musing, with her eyes on the fire, and he watches her in silence.) Paul, do you remember the deserted garden we sometimes used to walk in ?

Ventnor. —The old garden with the high wall at the end of the village street ? The garden with the ruined box-borders and the broken-down arbour ? Why, I remember every weed in the paths and every patch of moss on the walls!

Mrs Dale. —Well—I went back there the other day. The village is immensely improved. There's a new hotel with gas-fires, and a trolley in the main street; and the garden has been turned into a public park, where excursionists sit on
cast-iron benches admiring the statue of an Abolitionist.

Ventnor. — An Abolitionist—how appropriate !

Mrs Dale. —And the man who sold the garden has made a fortune that he doesn't know how to spend

Ventnor (rising impulsively). —Helen (he approaches and lays his hand on her letters), let's sacrifice our fortune and keep the excursionists out!

Mrs Dale (with a responsive movement). —Paul, do you really mean it ?

Ventnor (gaily). —Mean it? Why, I feel like a landed proprietor already! It's more than a garden—it's a park.

Mrs Dale. —It's more than a park, it's a world—as long as we keep it to ourselves !

Ventnor. —Ah, yes—even the pyramids look small when one sees a Cook's tourist on top of them! (He takes the key from the table, unlocks the cabinet and brings out his letters, which he lays beside hers.) Shall we burn the key to our garden ?

Mrs Dale. —Ah, then it will indeed be boundless! (Watching him while he throws the letters into the fire.)

Ventnor (turning back to her with a half-sad smile). — But not too big for us to find each other in ?

Mrs Dale. — Since we shall be the only people there! (He takes both her hands and they look at each other a moment in silence. Then he goes out by the door to the right. As he reaches the door she takes a step toward him impulsively; then turning back she leans against the chimney-piece, quietly watching the letters burn.)

THE REMBRANDT

THE REMBRANDT

" YOU'RE 50 artistic," my cousin Eleanor Copt began.

Of all Eleanor's exordiums it is the one I most dread. When she tells me I'm so clever I know this is merely the preamble to inviting me to meet the last literary obscurity of the moment: a trial to be evaded or endured, as circumstances dictate; whereas her calling me artistic fatally connotes the request to visit, in her company, some distressed gentlewoman whose future hangs on my valuation of her old Saxe or of her grandfather's Marc Antonios. Time was when I attempted to resist these compulsions of Eleanor's; but I soon learned that, short of actual flight, there was no refuge from her beneficent despotism. It is not always easy for the curator of a museum
to abandon his post on the plea of escaping a pretty cousin's importunities; and Eleanor, aware of my predicament, is none too magnanimous to take advantage of it. Magnanimity is, in fact, not in Eleanor's line. The virtues, she once explained to me, are like bonnets: the very ones that look best on other people may not happen to suit one's own particular style; and she added, with a slight deflection of metaphor, that none of the ready-made virtues ever had fitted her: they all pinched somewhere, and she'd given up trying to wear them.

Therefore when she said to me, " You're so artistic," emphasizing the conjunction with a tap of her dripping umbrella (Eleanor is out in all weathers: the elements are as powerless against her as man), I merely stipulated, " It's not old Saxe again ?"

She shook her head reassuringly. " A picture—a Rembrandt ! "

" Good Lord ! Why not a Leonardo ? "

" Well "—she smiled—" that, of course, depends on you"

"On me?"

" On your attribution. I dare say Mrs
Fontage would consent to the change — though she's very conservative."

A gleam of hope came to me and I pronounced: " One can't judge of a picture in this weather."

" Of course not. I'm coming for you to-morrow."

" I've an engagement to-morrow."

" I'll come before or after your engagement."

The afternoon paper lay at my elbow and I contrived a furtive consultation of the weather-report. It said, "Rain tomorrow," and I answered briskly: "All right, then; come at ten"—rapidly calculating that the clouds on which I counted might lift by noon.

My ingenuity failed of its due reward; for the heavens, as if in league with my cousin, emptied themselves before morning, and punctually at ten Eleanor and the sun appeared together in my office.

I hardly listened, as we descended the Museum steps and got into Eleanor's hansom, to her vivid summing-up of the case. I guessed beforehand that the lady we were about to visit had lapsed by the most distressful degrees from opulence to
a " hall-bedroom "; that her grandfather, if he had not been Minister to France, had signed the Declaration of Independence ; that the Rembrandt was an heirloom, sole remnant of disbanded treasures ; that for years its possessor had been unwilling to part with it, and that even now the question of its disposal must be approached with the most diplomatic obliquity.

Previous experience had taught me that all Eleanor's " cases " presented a harrowing similarity of detail. No circumstance tending to excite the spectator's sympathy and involve his action was omitted from the history of her beneficiaries ; the lights and shades were indeed so skilfully adjusted that any impartial expression of opinion took on the hue of cruelty. I could have produced closetfuls of "heirlooms " in attestation of this fact; for it is one more mark of

Eleanor's competence that her friends usually pay the interest on her philanthropy. My one hope was that in this case the object, being a picture, might reasonably be rated beyond my means; and as our cab drew up before a blistered brown-stone door-step I formed the self-defensive resolve to place an extreme valuation on Mrs Fontage's Rembrandt. It is Eleanor's fault if she is sometimes fought with her own weapons.

The house stood in one of those shabby provisional-looking New York streets that seem resignedly awaiting demolition. It was the kind of house that, in its high days, must have had a bow-window with a bronze in it. The bow-window had been replaced by a plumber's devanture, and one might conceive the bronze to have gravitated to the limbo where Mexican onyx tables and bric-a-brac in buffalo horn await the first signs of our next aesthetic reaction.

Eleanor swept me through a hall that smelled of poverty, up unlit stairs to a bare slit of a room. " And she must leave this in a month!" she whispered across her knock.

I had prepared myself for the limp widow's weed of a woman that one figures in such a setting; and confronted abruptly with Mrs Fontage's white-haired erect-ness I had the disconcerting sense that I was somehow in her presence at my own solicitation. I instinctively charged Eleanor with this reversal of the situation ; but a moment later I saw it must be ascribed to a something about Mrs Fontage that precluded the possibility of her asking any one a favour. It was not that she was of forbidding, or even majestic, demeanour; but that one guessed, under her aquiline prettiness, a dignity nervously on guard against the petty betrayal of her surroundings. The room was unconcealably poor; the little faded " relics," the high-stocked ancestral silhouettes, the steel engravings after Raphael and Correggio, grouped in a vain attempt to hide the most obvious stains on the wall-paper, served only to accentuate the contrast of a past evidently diversified by foreign travel and the enjoyment of the arts. Even Mrs Fontage's dress had the air of being a last expedient, the ultimate outcome of a much-taxed ingenuity in darning and turning. One felt that all the poor lady's barriers were falling save that of her impregnable manner.

To this manner I found myself conveying my appreciation of being admitted to a view of the Rembrandt.

THE REMBRANDT

Mrs Fontage's smile took my homage for granted. " It is always," she conceded, " a privilege to be in the presence of the great masters." Her slim wrinkled hand waved me to a dusky canvas near the window.

" It's so interesting, dear Mrs Fontage," I heard Eleanor exclaiming, "and my cousin will be able to tell you exactly "

Eleanor, in my presence, always admits that she knows nothing about art; but she gives the impression that this is merely because she hasn't had time to look into the matter—and has had me to do it for her.

Mrs Fontage seated herself without speaking, as though fearful that a breath might disturb my communion with the masterpiece. I felt that she thought Eleanor's reassuring ejaculations ill-timed; and in this I was of one mind with her; for the impossibility of telling her exactly what I thought of her Rembrandt had become clear to me at a glance.

My cousin's vivacities began to languish, and the silence seemed to shape itself into a receptacle for my verdict. I stepped back, affecting a more distant scrutiny; and as I did so my eye caught Mrs Fontage's profile. Her lids trembled slightly. I took refuge in the familiar expedient of asking the history of the picture, and she waved me brightly to a seat.

This was indeed a topic on which she could dilate. The Rembrandt, it appeared, had come into Mr Fontage's possession many years ago, while the young couple were on their wedding-tour, and under circumstances so romantic that she made no excuse for relating them in all their parenthetic fulness. The picture belonged to an old Belgian Countess of redundant quarterings, whom the extravagances of an ungovernable nephew had compelled to part with her possessions (in the most private manner) about the time of the Fontages' arrival. By a really remarkable coincidence, it happened that their courier (an exceptionally intelligent and superior man) was an old servant of the Countess's, and had thus been able to put them in the way of securing the Rembrandt under the very nose of an English Duke, whose agent had been sent to Brussels to negotiate for its purchase.

Mrs Fontage could not recall the Duke's name, but he was a great collector, and had a famous Highland castle, where somebody had been murdered, and which she herself had visited (by moonlight) when she had travelled in Scotland as a girl. The episode had in short been one of the most interesting " experiences " of a tour, almost chromo-lithographic in vivacity of impression; and they had always meant to go back to Brussels for the sake of re-living so picturesque a moment. Circumstances (of which the narrator's surroundings declare the nature) had persistently interfered with the projected return to Europe, and the picture had grown doubly valuable as representing the high-water mark of their artistic emotions. Mrs Fontage's moist eye caressed the canvas. " There is only," she added with a perceptible effort, " one slight drawback : the picture is not signed. But for that the Countess, of course, would have sold it to a museum. All the connoisseurs who have seen it pronounce it an undoubted Rembrandt, in the artist's best manner; but the museums" —she arched her brows in smiling recog-

nition of a well-known weakness—"give the preference to signed examples-Mrs Fontage's words evoked so touching a vision of the young tourists of fifty years ago, entrusting to an accomplished and versatile courier the direction of their helpless zeal for art, that I lost sight for a moment of the point at issue. The old Belgian Countess, the wealthy Duke with a feudal castle in Scotland, Mrs Fontage's own maiden pilgrimage to Arthur's Seat and Holyrood, all the accessories of the naif transaction, seemed a part of that vanished Europe to which our young race carried its indiscriminate ardours, its tender romantic credulity: the legendary castellated Europe of keepsakes, brigands and old masters, that compensated, by one such " experience " as Mrs Fontage's, for an after-life of aesthetic privation.

I was restored to the present by Eleanor's looking at her watch. The action mutely conveyed that something was expected of me. I risked the temporising statement that the picture was very interesting; but Mrs Fontage's polite assent revealed the poverty of the expedient. Eleanor's impatience overflowed.

I

" You would like my cousin to give you mi idea of its value ? " she suggested.

Mrs Fontage grew more erect. "No one," she corrected with great gentleness, " can know its value quite as well as I, who live with it—

We murmured our hasty concurrence.

"But it might be interesting to hear"—she addressed herself to me—"as a mere matter of curiosity—what estimate would be put on it from the purely commercial point of view—if such a term may be used in speaking of a work of art."

I sounded a note of deprecation.

"Oh, I understand, of course," she delicately anticipated me, "that that could never be your view, your personal view; but since occasions may arise—do arise—when it becomes necessary to—to put a price on the priceless, as it were — I have thought — Miss Copt has suggested "

"Some day," Eleanor encouraged her, " you might feel that the picture ought to belong to some one who has more— more opportunity of showing it—letting it be seen by the public—for educational reasons "

"I have tried," Mrs Fontage admitted, " to see it in that light."

The crucial moment was upon me. To escape the challenge of Mrs Fontage's brilliant composure I turned once more to the picture. If my courage needed reinforcement, the picture amply furnished it. Looking at that lamentable canvas seemed the surest way of gathering strength to denounce it; but behind me, all the while, I felt Mrs Fontage's shuddering pride drawn up in a final effort of self-defence. I hated myself for my sentimental pejversion of the situation. Reason argued that it was more cruel to deceive Mrs Fontage than to tell her the truth; but that merely proved the inferiority of reason to instinct in situations involving any concession to the emotions. Along with her faith in the Rembrandt I must destroy not only the whole fabric of Mrs Fontage's past, but even that life-long habit of acquiescence in untested formulas that makes the best part of the average feminine strength. I guessed the episode of the picture to be inextricably interwoven with the traditions and convictions which

served to veil Mrs Pontage's destitution not only from others but from herself. Viewed in that light the Rembrandt had perhaps been worth its purchase-money; and I regretted that works of art do not commonly sell on the merit of the moral support they may have rendered.

From this unavailing flight I was recalled by the sense that something must be done. To place a fictitious value on the picture was at best a provisional measure; while the brutal alternative of advising Mrs Fontage to sell it for a hundred dollars at least afforded an opening to the charitably disposed purchaser. I intended, if other resources failed, to put myself forward in that light; but delicacy of course forbade my coupling my unflattering estimate of the Rembrandt with an immediate offer to buy it. All I could do was to inflict the wound: the healing unguent must be withheld for later application.

I turned to Mrs Fontage, who sat motionless, her finely-lined cheeks touched with an expectant colour, her eyes averted from the picture which was so evidently the one object they beheld.

" My dear madam " I began. Her

vivid smile was like a light held up to dazzle me. It shrouded every alternative in darkness, and I had the flurried sense of having lost my way among the intricacies of my contention. Of a sudden I felt the hopelessness of finding a crack in her impenetrable conviction. My words slipped from me like broken weapons. "The picture," I faltered, "would of course be worth more if it were signed. As it is, I—I hardly think —on a conservative estimate—it can be valued at—at more—than—a thousand dollars, say "

My deflected argument ran on somewhat aimlessly till it found itself plunging full tilt against the barrier of Mrs Fontage's silence. She sat as impassive as though I had not spoken. Eleanor loosed a few fluttering words of congratulation and encouragement, but their flight was suddenly cut short. Mrs Fontage had risen with a certain solemnity.

" I could never," she said gently—her gentleness was adamantine—"under any circumstances whatever, consider, for a moment even, the possibility of parting with the picture at such a price."

n

WITHIN three weeks a tremulous note from Mrs Fontage requested the favour of another visit. If the writing was tremulous, however, the writer's tone was firm. She named her own day and hour, without the conventional reference to her visitor's convenience.

My first impulse was to turn the note over to Eleanor. I had acquitted myself of my share in the ungrateful business of coming to Mrs Fontage's aid, and if, as her letter denoted, she had now yielded to the closer pressure of need, the business of finding a purchaser for the Rembrandt might well be left to my cousin's ingenuity. But here conscience put in the uncomfortable reminder that it was I who, in putting a price on the picture, had raised the real obstacle in the way of Mrs Fontage's rescue. No one would give a thousand dollars for the Rembrandt ; but to tell Mrs Fontage so had become as unthinkable as murder, I

had, hi fact, on returning from my first inspection of the picture, refrained from imparting to Eleanor my opinion of its value. Eleanor is porous, and I knew that sooner or later the unnecessary truth would exude through the loose texture of her dissimulation. Not infrequently she thus creates the misery she alleviates ; and I have sometimes suspected her of paining people in order that she might be sorry for them. I had, at all events, cut off retreat in Eleanor's direction; and the remaining alternative carried me straight to Mrs Fontage.

She received me with the same commanding sweetness. The room was even barer than before—I believe the carpet was gone—but her manner built up about her a palace to which I was welcomed with high state; and it was as a mere incident of the ceremony that I was presently made aware of her decision to sell the Rembrandt. My previous unsuccess in planning how to deal with Mrs Fontage had warned me to leave my farther course to chance; and I listened to her explanation with complete detachment. She had resolved to travel for her health; her doctor advised it, and as her absence might be indefinitely prolonged she had reluctantly decided to part with the picture in order to avoid the expense of storage and insurance. Her voice drooped at the admission, and she hurried on, detailing the vague itinerary of a journey that was to combine long-promised visits to impatient friends with various " interesting opportunities" less definitely specified. The poor lady's skill in rearing a screen of verbiage about her enforced avowal had distracted me from my own share in the situation, and it was with dismay that I suddenly caught the drift of her assumptions. She expected me to buy the Rembrandt for the Museum; she had taken my previous valuation as a tentative bid, and when I came to my senses she was in the act of accepting my offer.

Had I had a thousand dollars of my own to dispose of, the bargain would have been concluded on the spot; but I was in the impossible position of being materially unable to buy the picture, and morally unable to tell her that it was not worth acquiring for the Museum.

I dashed into the first evasion in sight.

I had no authority, I explained, to purchase pictures for the Museum without the consent of the Committee.

Mrs Fontage coped for a moment in silence with the incredible fact that I had rejected her offer; then she ventured, with a kind of pale precipitation: " But I understood—Miss Copt tells me that you practically decide such matters for the Committee." I could guess what the effort had cost her.

" My cousin is given to generalizations. My opinion may have some weight with the Committee "

" Well then " she timidly prompted.

" For that very reason I can't buy the picture."

She said, with a drooping note, " I don't understand."

"Yet you told me," I reminded her, "that you knew museums didn't buy unsigned pictures."

" Not for what they are worth ! Every one knows that. But I—I understood— the price you named— Her pride

shuddered back from the abasement. " It's a misunderstanding then," she faltered.

To avoid looking at her, I glanced desperately at the Rembrandt. Could I— —? But reason rejected the possibility. Even if the Committee had been blind— and they all were but Crozier—I simply shouldn't have dared to do it. I stood up, feeling that to cut the matter short was the only alleviation within reach.

Mrs Fontage had summoned her indomitable smile; but its brilliancy dropped, as I opened the door, like a candle blown out by a draught.

" If there's any one else—if you knew any one who would care to see the picture, I should be most happy " She kept

her eyes on me, and I saw that, in her case, it hurt less than to look at the Rembrandt. " I shall have to leave here, you know," she panted, "if nobody cares to have it "

in

'I ! i AT evening at my club I had just succeeded in losing sight of Mrs Fontage in the fumes of an excellent cigar, when a voice at my elbow evoked her harassing image.

" I want to talk to you," the speaker said, " about Mrs Fontage's Rembrandt."

" There isn't any," I was about to growl; but looking up I recognised the confiding countenance of Mr Jefferson Rose.

Mr Rose was known to me chiefly as a young man suffused with a vague enthusiasm for Virtue and my cousin Eleanor.

One glance at his glossy exterior conveyed the assurance that his morals were as immaculate as his complexion and his linen. Goodness exuded from his moist eye, his liquid voice, the warm damp pressure of his trustful hand. He had always struck me as one of the most uncomplicated organisms I had ever met. His ideas were as simple and inconsecutive as the propositions in a primer, and he spoke slowly, with a kind of uniformity of emphasis that made his words stand out like the raised type for the blind. An obvious incapacity for abstract conceptions made him peculiarly susceptible to the magic of generalization, and one felt he would have been at the mercy of any Cause that spelled itself with a capital letter. It was hard to explain how, with such a superabundance of merit, he

managed to be a good fellow : I can only say that he performed the astonishing feat as naturally as he supported an invalid mother and two sisters on the slender salary of a banker's clerk. He sat down beside me with an air of bright expectancy.

" It's a remarkable picture, isn't it ?" he said.

" You've seen it ?"

"I've been so fortunate. Miss Copt was kind enough to get Mrs Fontage's permission; we went this afternoon."

I inwardly wished that Eleanor had selected another victim; unless indeed the visit were part of the plan whereby some third person, better equipped for the cultivation of delusions, was to be made to think the Rembrandt remarkable. Knowing the limitations of Mr Rose's resources I began to wonder if he had any rich aunts.

" And her buying it in that way, too," he went on with his limpid smile, " from that old Countess in Brussels, makes it all the more interesting, doesn't it ? Miss Copt tells me it's very seldom old pictures can be traced back for more than a generation. I suppose the fact of Mrs Fontage's knowing its history must add a good deal to its value ?"

Uncertain as to his drift, I said: "In her eyes it certainly appears to."

Implications are lost on Mr Rose, who glowingly continued: " That's the reason why I wanted to talk to you about it — to consult you. Miss Copt tells me you value it at a thousand dollars."

There was no denying this, and I grunted a reluctant assent.

" Of course," he went on earnestly, " your valuation is based on the fact that the picture isn't signed—Mrs Fontage explained that; and it does make a difference, certainly. But the thing is— if the picture's really good—ought one to take advantage ? I mean—one can see that Mrs Fontage is in a tight place, and I wouldn't for the world "

My astonished stare arrested him.

" You wouldn't ?"

" I mean—you see, it's just this way " ; he coughed and blushed: "I can't give more than a thousand dollars myself— it's as big a sum as I can manage to scrape together—but before I make the offer I want to be sure I'm not standing in the way of her getting more money."

My astonishment lapsed to dismay. " You're going to buy the picture for a thousand dollars ?"

His blush deepened. "Why, yes. It sounds rather absurd, I suppose. It isn't much in my line, of course. I can see the picture's very beautiful, but I'm no judge — it isn't the kind of thing, naturally, that I could afford to go in for; but in this case I'm very glad to do what I can; the circumstances are so distressing; and knowing what you think of the picture I feel it's a pretty safe investment "

" I don't think!" I blurted out.

"You ?"

" I don't think the picture's worth a thousand dollars; I don't think it's worth ten cents; I simply lied about it, that's all."

Mr Rose looked as frightened as though I had charged him with the offence.

" Hang it, man, can't you see how it happened? I saw the poor woman's pride and happiness hung on her faith in that picture. I tried to make her understand that it was worthless—but she wouldn't; I tried to tell her so—but I couldn't. I behaved like a maudlin ass, but you shan't pay for my infernal bungling—you mustn't buy the picture."

Mr Rose sat silent, tapping one glossy boot-tip with another. Suddenly he turned on me a glance of stored intelligence. " But you know," he said good - humouredly, " I rather think I must."

" You haven't already ?"

" Oh no ; the offer's not made."

"Well, then-

His look gathered a brighter significance.

" But if the picture's worth nothing, nobody will buy it

I groaned.

" Except," he continued, " some fellow like me, who doesn't know anything. / think it's lovely, you know; I mean to hang it in my mother's sitting-room." He rose and clasped my hand in his adhesive pressure. "I'm awfully obliged to you for telling me this; but perhaps you won't mind my asking you not to mention our talk to Miss Copt? It might bother her, you know, to think the picture isn't exactly up to the murk ; and it won't make a rap of difference to me."

IV

MR ROSE left me to a sleepless night. The next morning my resolve was fonned, and it carried me straight to Mrs Fontage's. She answered my knock by stepping out on the landing, and as she shut the door behind her I caught a glimpse of her devastated interior. She mentioned, with a careful avoidance of the note of pathos on which our last conversation had closed, that she was preparing to leave that afternoon; and the trunks obstructing the threshold showed that her preparations were nearly complete. They were, I felt certain, the same trunks that, strapped behind a rattling vettura, had accompanied the bride and groom on that memorable voyage of discovery of which the booty had till recently adorned her walls; and there was a dim consolation in the thought that those early " finds" in coral and Swiss wood-carving, in lava and alabaster, still lay behind the worn locks, in the security of worthlessness.

Mrs Fontage, on the landing, among her strapped and corded treasures, maintained the same air of stability that made it impossible, even under such conditions, to regard her flight as anything less dignified than a departure. It was the moral support of what she tacitly assumed that enabled me to set forth with proper deliberation the object of my visit; and she received my announcement with an absence of surprise that struck me as the very flower of tact. Under cover of these mutual assumptions the transaction was rapidly concluded; and it was not till the canvas passed into my hands that, as though the physical contact had unnerved her, Mrs Fontage suddenly faltered. "It's the giving it up— she stammered, disguising herself to the last; and I hastened away from the collapse of her splendid effrontery.

I need hardly point out that I had acted impulsively, and that reaction from the most honourable impulses is sometimes attended by moral perturbation. My motives had indeed been mixed enough to justify some uneasiness, but this was allayed by the instinctive feeling that it is more venial to defraud an institution than a man. Since Mrs Fontage had to be kept from starving by means not wholly defensible, it was better that the obligation should be borne by a rich institution than an impecunious youth. I doubt, in fact, if my scruples would have survived a night's sleep, had they not been complicated by some uncertainty as to my own future. It was true that, subject to the purely formal assent of the Committee, I had full power to buy for the Museum, and that the one member of the Committee likely to dispute my decision was opportunely travelling in Europe; but the picture once in place I must face the risk of any expert criticism to which chance might expose it. I dismissed this contingency for future study, stored the Rembrandt in the cellar of the Museum, and thanked Heaven that Crozier was abroad.

Six months later he strolled into my office. I had just concluded, under conditions of exceptional difficulty, and

on terms unexpectedly benign, the purchase of the great Bartley Reynolds; and this circumstance, by relegating the matter of the Rembrandt to a lower stratum of consciousness, enabled me to welcome Crozier with unmixed pleasure. My security was enhanced by his appearance. His smile was charged with amiable reminiscences, and I inferred that his trip had put him in the humour to approve of everything, or at least to ignore what fell short of his approval. I had therefore no uneasiness in accepting his invitation to dine that evening. It is always pleasant to dine with Crozier, and never more so than when he is just back from Europe. His conversation gives even the food a flavour of the Cafe Anglais.

The repast was delightful, and it was not till we had finished a Camembert, which he must have brought over with him, that my host said, in a tone of after-dinner perfunctoriness: "I see you've picked up a picture or two since I left."

I assented. "The Bartley Reynolds seemed too good an opportunity to miss,

especially as the French Government was after it. I think we got it cheap—

" Connu, connu" said Crozier pleasantly. " I know all about the Reynolds. It was the biggest kind of a haul, and I congratulate you. Best stroke of business we've done yet. But tell me about the other picture—the Rembrandt."

" I never said it was a Rembrandt." I could hardly have said why, but I felt distinctly annoyed with Crozier.

" Of course not. There's * Rembrandt' on the frame, but I saw you'd modified it to * Dutch School'; I apologise." He paused, but I offered no explanation. " What about it ?" he went on. " Where did you pick it up?" As he leaned to the flame of the cigar-lighter his face seemed ruddy with enjoyment.

" I got it for a song," I said.

" A thousand, I think ?"

" Have you seen it ?" I asked abruptly.

" Went over the place this afternoon and found it in the cellar. Why hasn't it been hung, by the way ?"

I paused a moment. " I'm waiting—

"J " ?

" To have it varnished."

"Ah!" He leaned back and poured himself a second glass of Chartreuse. The smile he confided to its golden depths provoked me to challenge him with—

" What do you think of it ?"

"The Rembrandt?" He lifted his eyes from the glass. - "Just what you do."

" It isn't a Rembrandt."

"I apologise again. You call it, I believe, a picture of the same period ?"

"I'm uncertain of the period."

" H'm." He glanced appreciatively along his cigar. " What are you certain of?"

"That it's a damned bad picture," I said savagely.

He nodded. " Just so. That's all we wanted to know."

" We?"

"We—I—the Committee, in short. You see, my dear fellow, if you hadn't been certain it was a damned bad picture our position would have been a little awkward. As it is, my remaining duty—I ought to explain that in this matter I'm acting for the Committee—is as simple as it's agreeable."

"I'll be hanged," I burst out, "if I understand one word you're saying!"

He fixed me with a kind of cruel joyousness. "You will—you will," he assured me; "at least you'll begin to, when you hear that I've seen Miss Copt."

"Miss Copt?"

"And that she has told me under what conditions the picture was bought."

"She doesn't know anything about the conditions! That is," I added, hastening to restrict the assertion, "she doesn't know my opinion of the picture." I thirsted for five minutes with Eleanor.

"Are you quite sure?" Crozier took me up. "Mr Jefferson Rose does."

"Ah—I see."

"I thought you would," he reminded me. "As soon as I'd laid eyes on the Rembrandt—I beg your pardon!—I saw that it—well, required some explanation."

"You might have come to me."

"I meant to; but I happened to meet Miss Copt, whose encyclopaedic information has often before been of service to me. I always go to Miss Copt when I want to look up anything: and I found she knew all about the Rembrandt."

"All?"

"Precisely. The knowledge was in fact causing her sleepless nights. Mr Rose, who was suffering from the same form of insomnia, had taken her into his confidence, and she, ultimately, took me into hers."

"Of course!"

"I must ask you to do your cousin justice. She didn't speak till it became evident to her uncommonly quick perceptions that your buying the picture on its merits would have been infinitely worse for—for everybody—than your diverting a small portion of the Museum's funds to philanthropic uses. Then she told me the moving incident of Mr Rose. Good fellow, Rose. And the old lady's case was desperate. Somebody had to buy that picture." I moved uneasily in my seat. "Wait a moment, will you? I haven't finished my cigar. There's a little head of Il Fiammingo's that you haven't seen, by the way; I picked it up the other day in Parma. We'll go in and have a look at it presently. But meanwhile what I want to say is, that I've been charged in the most informal way to express to you the Committee's appreciation of your admirable promptness and energy in capturing the Bartley Reynolds. We shouldn't have got it at all if you hadn't been uncommonly wide-awake, and to get it at such a price is a double triumph. We'd have thought nothing of a few more thousands—"

"I don't see," I impatiently interposed, "that, as far as I'm concerned, that alters the case."

"The case?"

"Of Mrs Pontage's Rembrandt. I bought the picture because, as you say, the situation was desperate, and I couldn't raise a thousand myself. What I did was of course, indefensible; but the money shall be refunded to-morrow—"

Crozier raised a protesting hand. "Don't interrupt me when I'm talking ex cathe-drd. The money's been refunded already. The fact is, the Museum has sold the Rembrandt."

I stared at him wildly. " Sold it ? To whom ?"

" Why—to the Committee. Hold on a bit, please. Won't you take another cigar ? Then perhaps I can finish what I've got to say. AVhy, my dear fellow, the Committee's

under an obligation to you—that's the way we look at it. I've investigated Mrs Fontage's case, and, well, the picture had to be bought. She's eating meat now, I believe, for the first time in a year. And they'd have turned her out into the street that very day, your cousin tells me. Something had to be done at once, and you've simply given a number of well-to-do and self-indulgent gentlemen the opportunity of performing, at very small individual expense, a meritorious action in the nick of time. That's the first thing I've got to thank you for. And then you'll remember, please, that I have the floor—that I'm still speaking for the Committee—and secondly, as a slight recognition of your services in securing the Bartley Reynolds at a very much lower figure than we were prepared to pay, we beg you—the Committee begs you—to accept the gift of Mrs Fontage's Rembrandt. Now we'll go in and look at that little head. .''

THE MOVING FINGER

VI THE MOVING FINGER

HT^HE news of Mrs Grancy's death came to me with the shock of an immense blunder—one of fate's most irretrievable acts of vandalism. It was as though all sorts of renovating forces had been checked by the clogging of that one wheel. Not that Mrs Grancy contributed any perceptible momentum to the social machine : her unique distinction was that of filling to perfection her special place in the world. So many people are like badly-composed statues, overlapping their niches at one point and leaving them vac-ant at another. Mrs Grancy's niche was her husband's life; and if it be argued that the space was not large enough for its vacancy to leave a very big gap, I can only say that, at the last resort, such

dimensions must be determined by finer instruments than any ready-made standard of utility. Ralph Grancy's was, in short, a kind of disembodied usefulness : one of those constructive influences that, instead of crystallising into definite forms, remain as it were a medium for the development of clear thinking and fine feeling. He faithfully irrigated his own dusty patch of life, and the fruitful moisture stole far beyond his boundaries. If, to carry on the metaphor, Grancy's life was a sedulously-cultivated enclosure, his wife was the flower he had planted in its midst —the embowering tree, rather, which gave him rest and shade at its foot and the wind of dreams in its upper branches. We had all—his small but devoted band of followers—known a moment when it seemed likely that Grancy would fail us. We had watched him pitted against one stupid obstacle after another —ill-health, poverty, misunderstanding, and, worst of all for a man of his texture, his first wife's soft insidious egotism. We had seen him sinking under the leaden embrace of her affection like a swimmer in a drowning clutch; but just as we despaired he had always come to the surface again, blinded, panting, but striking out fiercely for the shore. When at last her death released him it became a question as to how much of the man she had carried with her. Left alone, he revealed numb withered patches, like a tree from which a parasite has been stripped. Hut gradually he began to put out new leaves; and when he met the lady who was to become his second wife —his one real wife, as his friends reckoned —the whole man burst into flower.

The second Mrs Grancy was past thirty when he married her, and it was clear that she had harvested that crop of middle joy which is rooted in young despair. But if she had lost the surface of eighteen she had kept its inner light; if her cheek lacked the gloss of immaturity her eyes were young with the stored youth of half a life-time. Grancy had first known her somewhere in the East— I believe she was the sister of one of our consuls out there —and when he brought her home to New York she came among us as a stranger. The idea of Grancy's remarriage had been a shock to us all. After one such calcin-

ing most men would have kept out of the fire; but we agreed that he was predestined to sentimental blunders, and we awaited with resignation the embodiment of his latest mistake. Then Mrs Grancy came—and we understood. She was the most beautiful and the most complete of explanations. We shuffled our defeated omniscience out of sight, and gave it hasty burial under a prodigality of welcome. For the first time in years we had Grancy off our minds. " He'll do something great now!" the least sanguine of us prophesied; and our sentimentalist emended : " He has done it—in marrying her! "

It was Clay don, the portrait-painter, who risked this hyperbole ; and who soon afterward, at the happy husband's request, perpared to defend it in a portrait of Mrs Grancy. We were all—even Claydon— ready to concede that Mrs Grancy's un-wontedness was in some degree a matter of environment. Her graces were complementary, and it needed the mate's call to reveal the flash of colour beneath her neutral-tinted wings. But if she needed Grancy to interpret her, how much

greater was the service she rendered him ! Claydon professionally described her as the right frame for him ; but if she defined she also enlarged, if she threw the whole into perspective she also cleared new ground, opened fresh vistas, reclaimed whole areas of activity that had run to waste under the harsh husbandry of privation. This interaction of sympathies was not without its visible expression. Claydon was not alone in maintaining that Grancy's presence—or indeed the mere mention of his name—had a perceptible effect on his wife's appearance. It was as though a light were shifted, a curtain drawn back, as though, to borrow another of Claydon's metaphors, Love the indefatigable artist were perpetually seeking a happier "pose " for his model. In this interpretative light Mrs Grancy acquired the charm which makes some women's faces like a book of which the last page is never turned. There was always something new to read in her eyes. What Claydon read there—or at least such scattered hints of the ritual as reached him through the sanctuary doors —his portrait in due course declared to us,

When the picture was exhibited it was at once acclaimed as his masterpiece ; but the people who knew Mrs Grancy smiled and said it was flattered. Claydon, however, had not set out to paint their Mrs Grancy—or ours even—but Ralph's ; and Ralph knew his own at a glance. At the first confrontation he saw that Claydon had understood. As for Mrs Grancy, when the finished picture was shown to her, she turned to the painter and said simply: " Ah, you've done me facing the east ! "

The picture, then, for all its value, seemed a mere incident in the unfolding of their double destiny, a footnote to the illuminated text of their lives. It was not till afterward that it acquired the significance of last words spoken on a threshold never to be recrossed. Grancy, a year after his marriage, had given up his town house and carried his bliss an hour's journey away, to a little place among the hills. His various duties and interests brought him frequently to New York, but we necessarily saw him less often than when his house had served as the rallying-point of kindred enthusiasms. It seemed a pity that such an influence

in

in our talk like a gleam of sky in the hurrying current, Claydon, averted from the real woman, would sit as it were listening to the picture. His attitude, at the time, seemed only a part of the un-usualness of those picturesque afternoons, when the most familiar combinations of life underwent a magical change. Some human happiness is a landlocked lake; but the Grancys' was an open sea, stretching a buoyant and illimitable surface to the voyaging interests of life. There was room and to spare on those waters for all our separate ventures; and always, beyond the sunset, a mirage of the fortunate isles toward which our prows were bent.

ii

IT was in Rome that, three years later, I heard of her death. The notice said " suddenly." I was glad of that. I was glad too—basely perhaps—to be away from Grancy at a time when silence must have seemed obtuse and speech derisive.

I was still in Rome when, a few onths afterward, he suddenly arrived there. He had been appointed Secretary of Legation at Constantinople, and was on the way to his post. He had taken the place, he said frankly, "to get away." Our relations with the Porte held out a prospect of hard work, and that, he explained, was what he needed. He could never be satisfied to sit down among the ruins. I saw that, like most of us in moments of extreme moral tension, he was playing a part, behaving as he thought it became a man to behave in the eye of disaster. The instinctive posture of grief is a shuffling compromise between defiance and prostration; and pride feels the need of striking a worthier attitude in face of such a foe. Grancy, by nature musing and retrospective, had chosen the rdle of the man of action, who answers blow for blow and opposes a mailed front to the thrusts of destiny; and the completeness of the equipment testified tD his inner weakness. We talked only of what we were not thinking of, and parted, after a few days, with a sense of relief that proved the inadequacy of friendship to perform, in such cases, the office assigned to it by tradition.

Soon afterward my own work called me home, but Grancy remained several years in Europe. International diplomacy kept its promise of giving him work to do, and during the year in which he acted as chargS d'affaires he acquitted himself, under trying conditions, with conspicuous zeal and discretion. A political redistribution of matter removed him from office just as he had proved his usefulness to the Government ; and the following summer I heard that he had come home and was down at his place in the country.

On my return to town I wrote him, and his reply came by the next post. He answered as it were in his natural voice, urging me to spend the following Sunday with him, and suggesting that I should bring down any of the old set who could be persuaded to join me. I thought this a good sign, and yet—shall I own it?— I was vaguely disappointed. Perhaps we are apt to feel that our friends' sorrows should be kept like those historic monuments from which the encroaching ivy is periodically removed.

That very evening at the club I ran across Claydon. I told him of Grancy's invitation, and proposed that we should go down together; but he pleaded an engagement. I was sorry, for I had always felt that he and I stood nearer Ralph than the others, and if the old Sundays were to be renewed, I should have preferred that we two should spend the first alone with him. I said as much to Claydon, and offered to fit my time to his; but he met this by a general refusal.

" I don't want to go to Grancy's," he said bluntly. I waited a moment, but he appended no qualifying clause.

" You've seen him since he came back ?" I finally ventured.

Claydon nodded.

" And he is so awfully bad ?"

" Bad ? No : he's all right."

"All right? How can he be, unless he's changed beyond all recognition ?"

" Oh, you'll recognise him" said Claydon, with a puzzling deflection of emphasis,

His ambiguity was beginning to exasperate me, and I felt myself shut out from some knowledge to which I had as good a right as he.

" You've been down there already, I suppose ?"

" Yes ; I've been down there."

" And you've done with each other— the partnership is dissolved ?"

"Done with each other? I wish to God we had!" He rose nervously and tossed aside the review from which my approach had diverted him. " Look here," he said, standing before me, " Ralph's the best fellow going, and there's nothing under Heaven I wouldn't do for him—short of going down there again." And with that he walked out of the room.

Claydon was incalculable enough for me to read a dozen different meanings into his words; but none of my interpretations satisfied me. I determined, at any rate, to seek no farther for a companion ; and the next Sunday I travelled down to Grancy's alone. He met me at the station, and I saw at once that he had changed since our last meeting. Then he

had been in fighting array, but now if he and grief still housed together it was no longer as enemies. Physically, the transformation was as marked but less reassuring. If the spirit triumphed the body showed its scars. At five-and-forty he was grey and stooping, with the tired gait of an old man. His serenity, however, was not the resignation of age. I saw that he did not mean to drop out of the game. Almost immediately he began to speak of our old interests; not with an effort, as at our former meeting, but simply and naturally, in the tone of a man whose life has flowed back into its normal channels. I remembered, with a touch of self-reproach, how I had distrusted his reconstructive powers; but my admiration for his reserved force W.MS now tinged by the sense that, after all, such happiness as his ought to have been paid with his last coin. The feeling grew as we neared the house, and I found how inextricably his wife was interwoven with my remembrance of the place: how the whole scene was but an extension of that vivid presence.

Within doors nothing was changed,

and my hand would have dropped without surprise into her welcoming clasp. It was luncheon-time, and Grancy led me at once to the dining-room, where the walls, the furniture, the very plate and porcelain, seemed a mirror in which a moment since her face had been reflected. I wondered whether Grancy, under the recovered tranquillity of his smile, concealed the same sense of her nearness, saw perpetually between himself and the actual her bright unappeasable ghost. He spoke of her once or twice, in an easy incidental way, and her name seemed to hang in the air after he had uttered it like a chord that continues to vibrate. If he felt her presence it was evidently as an enveloping medium, the moral atmosphere in which he breathed. I had never before known how completely the dead may survive.

After luncheon we went for a long walk through the autumnal fields and woods, and dusk was falling when we re-entered the house. Grancy led the way to the library, where, at this hour, his wife had always welcomed us back to a bright fire and a cup of tea. The room faced the

west, and held a clear light of its own after the rest of the house had grown dark. I remembered how young she had looked in this pale gold light, which irradiated her eyes and hair, or silhouetted her girlish outline as she passed before the windows. Of all the rooms the library was most peculiarly hers; and here I felt that her nearness might take visible shape. Then, all in a moment, as Grancy opened the door, the feeling vanished and a kind of resistance met me on the threshold. I looked about me. Was the room changed ? Had some desecrating hand effaced the traces of her presence ? No; here too the setting was undisturbed. My feet sank into the same deep-piled Daghestan ; the book-shelves took the firelight on the same rows of rich subdued bindings; her armchair stood in its old place near the tea-table ; and from the opposite wall her face confronted me.

Her face—but ivas it hers ? I moved nearer and stood looking up at the portrait. Grancy's glance had followed mine, and 1 heard him move to my side.

" You see a change in it ?" he said.

" What does it mean ?" I asked.

" It means—that five years have passed."

"Over^er?"

"Why not? Look at me!" He pointed to his grey hair and furrowed temples. " What do you think kept her so young ? It was happiness! But now " he looked up at her with infinite tenderness. " I like her better so," he said. " It's what she would have wished."

" Have wished ? "

"That we should grow old together. Do you think she would have wanted to be left behind ?"

I stood speechless, my gaze travelling from his worn grief-beaten features to the painted face above. It was not furrowed like his ; but a veil of years seemed to have descended on it. The bright hair had lost its elasticity, the cheek its clearness, the brow its light: the whole woman had waned.

Grancy laid his hand on my arm. " You don't like it ?" he said sadly,

"Like it? I—I've lost her!" I burst out.

" And I've found her," he answered.

" In that ?" I cried with a reproachful gesture.

"Yes; in that." He swung round on me almost defiantly. " The other had become a sham, a lie! This is the way she would have looked—does look, I mean. Claydon ought to know, oughtn't he?"

I turned suddenly. " Did Claydon do this for you ?"

Grancy nodded.

" Since your return ?"

"Yes. I sent for him after I'd been back a week— He turned away and

gave a thrust to the smouldering fire. I followed, glad to leave the picture behind me. Grancy threw himself into a chair near the hearth, so that the light fell on his sensitive, variable face. He leaned his head back, shading his eyes with his hand, and began to speak.

in

" You fellows knew enough of my early history to guess what my second marriage meant to me. I say guess, because no one could understand—really. I've always o

had a feminine streak in me, I suppose: the need of a pair of eyes that should see with me, of a pulse that should keep time with mine. Life is a big thing, of course; a magnificent spectacle; but I got so tired of looking at it alone! Still it's always good to live, and I had plenty 'of happiness—of the evolved kind. What I'd never had a taste of was the simple inconscient sort that one breathes in like the air. . .

" Well—I met her. It was like finding the climate in which I was meant to live. You know what she was—how indefinitely she multiplied one's points of contact with life, how she lit up the caverns and bridged the abysses ! Well, I swear to you (though I suppose the sense of all that was latent in me) that what I used to think of on my way home at the end of the day was simply that when I opened this door she'd be sitting over there, with the lamplight falling in a particular way on one little curl in her neck. . . When Claydon painted her he caught just the look she used to lift to mine when I came in—I've wondered, sometimes, at his knowing how she looked when she and I were alone.—

How I rejoiced in that picture! I used to say to her, ' You're my prisoner now— I shall never lose you. If you grew tired of me and left me you'd leave your real self there on the wall!' It was always one of our jokes that she was going to grow tired of me

" Three years of it—and then she died. It was so sudden that there was no change, no diminution. It was as if she had suddenly become fixed, immovable, like her own portrait: as if time had ceased at its happiest hour, just as Claydon had thrown down his brush one day and said, 4 1 can't do better than that.'

" I went away, as you know, and stayed over there five years. I worked as hard as I knew how, and after the first black months a little light stole in on me. From thinking that she would have been interested in what I was doing I came to feel that she was interested—that she was there and that she knew. I'm not talking any psychical jargon—I'm simply tiying to express the sense I had that an influence so full, so abounding as hers, couldn't pass like a spring shower. We had so lived into each other's hearts and minds

that the consciousness of what she would have thought and felt illuminated all I did. At first she used to come back shyly, tentatively, as though not sure of finding me; then she stayed longer and longer, till at last she became again the very air I breathed. . . There were bad moments, of course, when her nearness mocked me with the loss of the real woman; but gradually the distinction between the two was effaced and the mere thought of her grew warm as flesh and blood.

" Then I came home. I landed in the morning and came straight down here. The thought of seeing her portrait possessed me, and my heart beat like a lover's as I opened the library door. It was in the afternoon and the room was full of light. It fell on her picture—the picture of a young and radiant woman. She smiled at me coldly across the distance that divided us. I had the feeling that she didn't even recognise me. And then I caught sight of myself in the mirror over there—a grey-haired broken man whom she had never known !

" For a week we two lived together—

the strange woman and the strange man. I used to sit night after night and question her smiling face ; but no answer ever came. What did she know of me, after all ? We were irrevocably separated by the five years of life that lay between us. At times, as I sat here, I almost grew to hate her; for her presence had driven away my gentle ghost, the real wife who had wept, aged, struggled with me during those awful years. . . It was the worst loneliness I've ever known. Then, gradually, I began to notice a look of sadness in the picture's eyes; a look that seemed to say : ' Don't you see that / am lonely too?' And all at once it came over me how she would have hated to be left behind ! I remembered her comparing life to a heavy book that could not be read with ease unless two people held it together; and I thought how impatiently her hand would have turned the pages that divided us !—So the idea came to me: ' It's the picture that stands between us ; the picture that is dead, and not my wife. To sit in this room is to keep watch beside a corpse.' As this feeling grew on me the portrait became

like a beautiful mausoleum in which she had been buried alive: I could hear her beating against the painted walls and crying to me faintly for help. .

" One day I found I couldn't stand it any longer and I sent for Claydon. He came down and I told him what I'd been through, and what I wanted him to do. At first he refused point-blank to touch the picture. The next morning I went off for a long tramp, and when I came home I found him sitting here alone. He looked at me sharply for a moment, and then he said: * I've changed my mind; I'll do it.' I arranged one of the north rooms as a studio, and he shut himself up there for a day; then he sent for me. The picture stood there as you see it now—it was as though she'd met me on the threshold and taken me in her arms! I tried to thank him, to tell him what it meant to me, but he cut me short.

" ' There's an up - train at five, isn't there ?' he asked. ' I'm booked for a dinner to-night. I shall just have time to make a bolt for the station, and you can send my traps after me.' I haven't seen him since.

" I can guess what it cost him to lay hands on his masterpiece; but, after all, to him it was only a picture lost, to me it was my wife regained !"

IV

AFTER that, for ten years or more, I watched the strange spectacle of a life of hopeful and productive effort based on the structure of a dream. There could be no doubt to those who saw Grancy during this period that he drew his strength and courage from the sense of his wife's mystic participation in his task. When I went back to see him a few months later I found the portrait had been removed from the library and placed in a small study upstairs, to which he had transferred his desk and a few books. He told me he always sat there when he was alone, keeping the library for his Sunday visitors. Those who missed the portrait of course made no comment on its absence, and the few who were in his secret respected it. Gradually all his old friends had gathered about him, and our Sunday afternoons regained something of their

former character; but Claydon never reappeared among us.

As I look back now I see that Grancy must have been failing from the time of his return home. His invincible spirit belied and disguised the signs of weakness that afterward asserted themselves in my remembrance of him. He seemed to have an inexhaustible fund of life to draw on, and more than one of us was a pensioner on his superfluity.

Nevertheless, when I came back one summer from my European holiday and heard that he had been at the point of death, I understood at once that we had believed him well only because he wished us to.

I hastened down to the country and found him midway in a slow convalescence. I felt then that he was lost to us, and he read my thought at a glance.

" Ah," he said, "I'm an old man now, and no mistake. I suppose we shall have to go half-speed after this; but we shan't need towing just yet!"

The plural pronoun struck me, and involuntarily I looked^ up at Mrs Grancy's portrait. Line by line I saw my fear

reflected in it. It was the face of a woman who knows that her husband is dying. My heart stood still at the thought of what Claydon had done.

Grancy had followed my glance. " Yes, it's changed her," he said quietly. " For months, you know, it was touch and go with me—we had a long fight of it, and it was worse for her than for me." After a pause he added: " Claydon has been very kind; he's so busy nowadays that I seldom see him, but when I sent for him the other day he came down at once."

I was silent, and we spoke no more of Grancy's illness; but when I took leave it seemed like shutting him in alone with his death-warrant.

The next time I went down to see him he looked much better. It was a Sunday, and he received me in the library, so that I did not see the portrait again. He continued to improve, and towards spring we began to feel that, as he had said, he might yet travel a long way without being towed.

One evening, on returning to town after a visit which had confirmed my sense of reassurance, I found Claydon dining alone at the club. He asked me to join him, and over the coffee our talk turned to his work.

"If you're not too busy," I said at length, " you ought to make time to go down to Grancy's again."

He looked up quickly. "Why?" he asked.

"Because he's quite well again," I returned, with a touch of cruelty. " His wife's prognostications were mistaken."

Claydon stared at me a moment. " Oh, she knows," he affirmed, with a smile that chilled me.

" You mean to leave the portrait as it is then ?" I persisted.

He shrugged his shoulders. "He hasn't sent for me yet!"

A waiter came up with the cigars, and Claydon rose and joined another group.

It was just a fortnight later that Grancy's housekeeper telegraphed for me. She met me at the station with the news that he had been "taken bad," and that the doctors were with him. I had to wait for some time in the deserted library before the medical men appeared. They had the baffled manner of empirics who have been superseded by the great Healer; and I lingered only long enough to hear that Grancy was not suffering, and that my presence could do him no harm.

I found him seated in his arm-chair in the little study. He held out his hand with a smile.

" You see she was right after all," he said.

"She?" I repeated, perplexed for the moment.

" My wife." He indicated the picture. " Of course I knew she had no hope from the first. I saw that"—he lowered his voice—" after Clay don had been here. But I wouldn't believe it at first!"

I caught his hands in mine. " For God's sake don't believe it now!" I adjured him.

He shook his head gently. " It's too lute," he said. " I might have known that she knew."

" But, Grancy, listen to me," I began; and then I stopped. What could I say that would convince him ? There was no common ground of argument on which we could meet; and after all it would be easier for him to die feeling that she had known. Strangely enough, I saw that Claydon had missed his mark. . . .

GRANCY'S will named me as one of his executors; and my associate, having other duties on his hands, begged me to assume the task of carrying out our friend's wishes. This placed me under the necessity of informing Claydon that the portrait of Mrs Grancy had been bequeathed to him; and he replied by the next post that he would send for the picture at once. I was staying in the deserted house when the portrait was taken away; and as the door closed on it I felt that Grancy's presence had vanished too. Was it his turn to follow her now, and could one ghost haunt another ?

After that, for a year or two, I heard nothing more of the picture, and though I met Claydon from time to time we had little to say to each other. I had no definable grievance against the man, and I tried to remember that he had done a fine thing in sacrificing his best picture to a friend; but my resentment had all the tenacity of unreason.

One day, however, a lady whose portrait he had just finished begged me to go with her to see it. To refuse was impossible, and I went with the less reluctance that I knew I was not the only friend she had invited. The others were all grouped around the easel when I entered, and after contributing my share to the chorus of approval I turned away and began to stroll about the studio. Claydon was something of a collector, and his things were generally worth looking at. The studio was a long tapestried room with a curtained archway at one end. The curtains were looped back, showing a smaller apartment, with books and flowers and a few fine bits of bronze and porcelain. The tea-table standing in this inner room proclaimed that it was open to inspection, and I wandered in. A bleu poudrt vase first attracted me; then I turned to

examine a slender bronze Ganymede, and in so doing found myself face to face with Mrs Grancy's portrait. I stared up at her blankly and she smiled back at me in all the recovered radiance of youth. The artist had effaced every trace of his later touches and the original picture had reappeared. It throned alone on the panelled wall, asserting a brilliant supremacy over its carefully-chosen surroundings. I felt in an instant that the whole room was tributary to it: that Claydon had heaped his treasures at the feet of the woman he loved. Yes —it was the woman he had loved and not the picture; and my instinctive resentment was explained.

Suddenly I felt a hand on my shoulder.

" Ah, how could you ?" I cried, turning on him.

" How could I ?" he retorted. " How could I not ? Doesn't she belong to me now ?"

I moved away impatiently.

"Wait a moment," he said with a detaining gesture. " The others have gone, and I want to say a word to you —Oh, I know what you've thought of

te—I can guess 1 You think I killed Grancy, I suppose ?"

I was startled by his sudden vehemence. " I think you tried to do a cruel thing," I said.

"Ah—what a little way you others see into life 1" he murmured. " Sit down a moment— here, where we can look at her—and I'll tell you."

He threw himself on the ottoman beside me and sat gazing up at the picture, with his hands clasped about his knee.

" Pygmalion," he began slowly, " turned his statue into a real woman; / turned my real woman into a picture. Small compensation, you think—but you don't know how much of a woman belongs to you after you've painted her!—Well, I made the best of it, at any rate—I gave her the best I had in me; and she gave me in return what such a woman gives by merely being. And after all, she rewarded me enough by making me paint as I shall never paint again ! There was one side of her, though, that was mine alone, and that was her beauty; for no one else understood it. To

Grancy even it was the mere expression of herself—what language is to thought. Even when he saw the picture he didn't guess my secret—he was so sure she was all his 1 As though a man should think he owned the moon because it was reflected in the pool at his door—

" Well—when he came home and sent for me to change the picture it was like asking me to commit murder. He wanted me to make an old woman of her—of her who had been so divinely, unchangeably young! As if any man who really loved a woman would ask her to sacrifice her youth and beauty for his sake! At first I told him I couldn't do it—but afterward, when he left me alone with the picture, something queer happened. I suppose it was because I was always so confoundedly fond of Grancy that it went against me to refuse what he asked. Anyhow, as I sat looking up at her, she seemed to say, ' I'm not yours but his, and I want you to make me what he wishes.' And so I did it. I could have cut my hand off when the work was done— I daresay he told you I never would go back and look at it.

He thought I was too busy—he never understood. . .

" Well—and then last year he sent for me again—you remember. It was after his illness, and he told me he'd grown twenty years older, and that he wanted her to grow older too—he didn't want her to be left behind. The doctors all thought he was going to get well at that time, and he thought so too; and so did I when I first looked at him. But when I turned to the picture— ah, now I don't ask you to believe me; but I swear it was her face that told me he was dying, and that she wanted him to know it! She had a message for him, and she made me deliver it."

He rose abruptly and walked toward the portrait; then he sat down beside me again.

" Cruel ? Yes, it seemed so, to me at first; and this time, if I resisted, it was for his sake and not for mine. But all the while I felt her eyes drawing me, and gradually she made me understand. If she'd been there in the flesh (she seemed to say) wouldn't she have seen before any of us that he was dying? p

CBUCTAL

Wouldn't he hare read the news first in her face? And wouldn't it be horrible if now he should discover it instead in strange eyes ?—Well—that was what she wanted of me and I did it—I kept them together to the last!" He looked up at the picture again. " But now she belongs to me,"" he repeated- . .

THE CONFESSIONAL

VII THE CONFESSIONAL

TI7HEN I was a young man I thought a great deal of local colour. At that time it was still a pigment of recent discovery, and supposed to have a peculiarly stimulating effect on the mental eye. As an aid to the imagination its value was perhaps overrated; but as an object of pursuit to that vagrant faculty, it had all the merits claimed for it. I certainly never hunted any game better worth my powder; and to a young man with rare holidays and long working hours, its value was enhanced by the fact that one might bring it down at any turn, if only one kept one's eye alert and one's hand on the trigger.

Even the large manufacturing city where, for some years, my young en-
thusiasms were chained to an accountant's desk, was not without its romantic opportunities. Many of the mill hands at Dunstable were Italians, and a foreign settlement had formed itself in that unsavoury and unsanitary portion of the town known as the Point. The Point, like more aristocratic communities, had its residential and commercial districts, its church, its theatre, and its restaurant. When the craving for local colour was on me it was my habit to resort to the restaurant, a low-browed wooden building with the appetizing announcement:

" Aristiu di montone"

pasted in one of its fly-blown window-panes. Here the consumption of tough macaroni or of an ambiguous frittura sufficed to transport me to the Cappello d'Oro in Venice, while my cup of coffee and a wasp-waisted cigar with a straw in it turned my greasy tablecloth into the marble top of one of the little round tables under the arcade of the Cafe Pedrotti at Padua, This feat of the imagination was materially aided by Agostino, the hollow-eyed and low-collared waiter, whose slimy napkin never lost its Latin flourish, and whose zeal for my comfort was not infrequently displayed by his testing the warmth of my soup with his finger. Through Agostino I became acquainted with the inner history of the colony, heard the details of its feuds and vendettas, and learned to know by sight the leading characters in these domestic dramas.

The restaurant was frequented by the chief personages of the community: the overseer of the Italian hands at the Meriton Mills, the doctor, his wife, the levatrice (a plump Neapolitan with greasy ringlets, a plush picture-hat, and a charm against the evil-eye hanging in a crease of her neck), and lastly by Don Egidio, the parocco of the little church across the street. The doctor and his wife came only on feast days, but the overseer and Don Egidio were regular patrons. The former was a quiet saturnine-looking man, of accomplished manners but reluctant speech, and I depended for my diversion chiefly on Don Egidio, whose large loosely-hung lips were always ajar for conversation. The remarks issuing

from them were richly tinged by the gutturals of the Bergamasque dialect, and it needed but a slight acquaintance with Italian types to detect the Lombard peasant under the priest's rusty cassock. This inference was confirmed by Don Egidio's telling me that he came from a village of Val Camonica, the radiant valley which extends northward from the lake of Iseo to the Adamello glaciers. His stepfather had been a labourer on one of the fruit farms of a Milanese count, who owned large estates in the Val Camonica; and that gentleman, taking a fancy to the lad, whom he had seen at work in his orchards, had removed him to his villa on the lake of Iseo, and had subsequently educated him for the Church.

It was doubtless to this picturesque accident that Don Egidio owed the mingling of ease and simplicity that gave an inimitable charm to his stout shabby presence. It was as though some wild mountain-fruit had been transplanted to the Count's orchards and had mellowed under cultivation without losing its sylvan flavour. I have never seen the social art carried farther without suggestion of

I

THE CONFESSIONAL 233

artifice. The fact that Don Egidio's amenities were mainly exercised on the mill hands composing his parish proved the genuineness of his gift. It is easier to simulate gentility among gentlemen than among navvies; and the plain man is a touchstone who draws out all the alloy in the gold.

Among his parishioners Don Egidio ruled with the cheerful despotism of the good priest. On cardinal points he was inflexible, but in minor matters he had that elasticity of judgment which enables the Catholic discipline to fit itself to every inequality of the human conscience. There was no appeal from his verdict; but his judgment-seat was a revolving chair from which he could view the same act at various angles. His influence was acknowledged not only by his flock, but by the policeman at the corner, the " bar-keep" in the dive, the ward politician in the corner grocery. The general verdict of Dunstable was that the Point would have been hell without the priest. It was perhaps not precisely heaven with him; but such light of the upper sky as pierced its murky atmosphere

was reflected from Don Egidio's countenance. It is hardly possible for any one to exercise such influence \\ithout taking pleasure in it; and on the whole the priest was probably a contented man, though it does not follow that he was a happy one. On this point the first stages of our acquaintance yielded much food for conjecture. At first sight Don Egidio was the image of cheerfulness. He had all the physical indications of a mind at ease : the leisurely rolling gait, the ready laugh, the hospitable eye of the man whose sympathies are always on the latch. It took me some time to discover under his surface garrulity the impenetrable reticence of his profession, and under his enjoyment of trifles a levelling melancholy which made all enjoyment trifling. Don Egidio's aspect and conversation were so unsugges-tive of psychological complexities that I set down this trait to poverty or homesickness. There are few classes of men more frugal in tastes and habit than the village priest in Italy; but Don Egidio, by his own account, had been introduced, at an impressionable age, to a way of living that must have surpassed his wildest dreams of self-indulgence. To whatever privations his parochial work had since accustomed him, the influences of that earlier life were too perceptible in his talk not to have made a profound impression on his tastes ; and he remained, for all his apostolic simplicity, the image of the family priest who has his seat at the rich man's table.

It chanced that I had used one of my short European holidays to explore a-foot the romantic passes connecting the Valtelline with the lake of Iseo; and my remembrance of that enchanting region made it seem impossible that Don Egidio should ever look without a reminiscent pang on the grimy perspective of his parochial streets. The transition was too complete, too ironical, from those rich glades and Titianesque acclivities to the brick hovels and fissured sidewalks of the Point.

This impression was confirmed when Don Egidio, in response to my urgent invitation, paid his first visit to my modest lodgings. He called one winter evening, when a wood fire in its happiest humour was giving a factitious lustre to my bookshelves and bringing out the values of the one or two old prints and Chinese porcelains that accounted for the perennial shabbiness of my wardrobe.

" Ah," said he with a murmur of satisfaction, as he laid aside his shiny hat and bulging umbrella, " it is a long time since I have been in a casa signorile"

My remembrance of his own room (he lodged with the doctor and the levatrice) saved this epithet from the suggestion of irony, and kept me silent while he sank into my arm-chair with the deliberation of a tired traveller lowering himself gently into a warm bath.

" Good ! good ! " he repeated, looking about him. " Books, porcelains, objects of virtu — I am glad to see that there are still such things in the world !" And he turned a genial eye on the glass of Marsala that I had poured out for him.

Don Egidio was the most temperate of men, and never exceeded his one glass; but he liked to sit by the hour puffing at my Cabanas, which I suspected him of preferring to the black weed of his native country. Under the influence of my tobacco he became even more blandly garrulous, and I sometimes fancied that of all the obligations of his calling none could have placed such a strain on him as that of preserving the secrets of the confessional. He often talked of his early life at the Count's villa, where he had been educated with his patron's two sons till he was of age to be sent to the seminary; and I could see that the years spent in simple and familiar intercourse with his benefactors had been the most vivid chapter in his experience. The Italian peasant's inarticulate tenderness for the beauty of his birthplace had been specialized in him by contact with cultivated tastes, and he could tell me not only that the Count had a " stupendous " collection of pictures, but that the chapel of the villa contained a sepulchral monument by Bambaja, and that the art critics were divided as to the authenticity of the Leonardo in the family palace at Milan.

On all these subjects he was inexhaustibly voluble; but there was one point which he always avoided, and that was his reason for coming to America. I remember the round turn with which he brought me up when I questioned him.

" A priest," said he, " is a soldier and must obey orders like a soldier." He set down his glass of Marsala and strolled across the room. " I had not observed," he went on, " that you have here a photograph of the Sposalizio of the Brera. What a picture! E stupendo/" and he turned back to his seat and smilingly lit a fresh cigar.

I saw at once that I had hit on a point where his native garrulity was protected by the chain-mail of religious discipline that every Catholic priest wears beneath his cassock. I had too much respect for my friend to wish to penetrate his armour, and now and then I almost fancied he was grateful to me for not putting his reticence to the test.

Don Egidio must have been past sixty when I made his acquaintance; but it was not till the close of an exceptionally harsh winter, some five or six years after our first meeting, that I began to think of him as an old man. It was as though the long-continued cold had cracked and shrivelled him. He had grown bent and hollow-chested and his lower lip shook like an unhinged door. The summer

heat did little to revive him, and in September, when I came home from my vacation, I found him just recovering from an attack of pneumonia. That autumn he did not care to venture often into the night air, and now and then I used to go and sit with him in his little room, to which I had contributed the unheard-of luxuries of an easy-chair and a gas-stove.

My engagements, however, made these visits infrequent, and several weeks had elapsed without my seeing the parocco when, one snowy November morning, I ran across him in the railway-station. I was on my way to New York for the day, and had just time to wave a greeting to him as I jumped into the railway-carriage; but a moment later, to my surprise, I saw him stiffly clambering into the same train. I found him seated in the common car, with his umbrella between his knees and a bundle done up in a red cotton handkerchief on the seat at his side. The caution with which, at my approach, he transferred this bundle to his arms caused me to glance at it in surprise; and he answered my look by saying with a smile :

" They are flowers for the dead—the most exquisite flowers—from the greenhouses of Mr Meriton— si figuri / " And he waved a descriptive hand. " One of my lads, Gianpietro, is employed by the gardener there, and every year on this day he brings me a beautiful bunch of flowers—for such a purpose it is no sin," he added, with the charming Italian pliancy of judgment.

"And why are you travelling in this snowy weather, signor parocco ? " I asked, as he ended with a cough.

He fixed me gravely with his simple shallow eye. "Because it is the day of the dead, my son," he said, " and I go to place these on the grave of the noblest man that ever lived."

" You are going to New York ?"

" To Brooklyn "

I hesitated a moment, wishing to question him, yet uncertain whether his replies were curtailed by the persistency of his cough or by the desire to avoid interrogation.

"This is no weather to be travelling with such a cough," I said at length.

He made a deprecating gesture.

" I have never missed the day—not once in eighteen years. But for me he would have no one !" He folded his hands on his umbrella, and looked away from me to hide the trembling of his lip.

I resolved on a last attempt to storm his confidence. " Your friend is buried in Calvary

Cemetery?"

He signed an assent.

"That is a long way for you to go alone, signor parocco. The streets are sure to be slippery, and there is an icy wind blowing. Give me your flowers, and let me send them to the cemetery by a messenger. I give you my word, they shall reach their destination safely."

He turned a quiet look on me. "My son, you are young," he said, "and you don't know how the dead need us." He drew his breviary from his pocket and opened it with a smile. "Mi scusi?" he murmured.

The business which had called me to town obliged me to part from him as soon as the train entered the station, and in my dash for the street I left his unwieldy figure labouring far behind me through the crowd on the platform. Before we separated, however, I had learned that he was returning to Dunstable by the four o'clock train, and had resolved to despatch my business in time to travel home with him. When I reached Wall Street, I was received with the news that the man I had appointed to meet was ill and detained in the country. My business was "off," and I found myself with the rest of the day at my disposal. I had no difficulty in deciding how to employ my time. I was at an age when, in such contingencies, there is always a feminine alternative; and even now I don't know how it was that, on my way to a certain hospitable luncheon-table, I suddenly found myself in a cab which was carrying me at full speed to the Twenty-third Street ferry. It was not till I had bought my ticket and seated myself in the varnished tunnel of the ferry-boat that I was aware of having been diverted from my purpose by an overmastering anxiety for Don Egidio. I rapidly calculated that he had not more than an hour's advance on me, and that, allowing for my greater agility and for the fact that I had a cab at my call, I was likely to reach the cemetery in time to see him under shelter before the gusts of sleet that were already sweeping across the river had thickened to a snowstorm.

At the gates of the cemetery I began to take a less sanguine view of my attempt. The commemorative anniversary had filled the silent avenues with visitors, and I felt the futility of my quest as I tried to fix the gatekeeper's attention on my delineation of a stout Italian priest with a bad cough and a bunch of flowers tied up in a red cotton handkerchief. The gatekeeper showed that delusive desire to oblige that is certain to send its victims in the wrong direction; but I had the presence of mind to go exactly contrary to his indication, and, thanks to this precaution, I came, after half-an-hour's search, on the figure of my poor parocco, kneeling on the wet ground in one of the humblest byways of the great necropolis. The mound before which he knelt was strewn with the spoils of Mr Meriton's conservatories, and on the weather-worn tablet at its head I read the inscription:

IL CONTE SIVIANO DA MILANO

Super flumina Babylonis, illie sedimus et flevimus

So engrossed was Don Egidio that for some moments I stood behind him unobserved; and when he rose and faced me, grief had left so little room for any minor emotion that he looked at me almost without surprise.

"Don Egidio," I said, "I have a carriage waiting for you at the gate. You must come home with me."

He nodded quietly, and I drew his hand through my arm.

He turned back to the grave. " One moment, my son," he said. " It may be for the last time." He stood motionless, his eyes on the heaped-up flowers which were already bruised and blackened by the cold. "To leave him alone—after

sixty years 1 But God is everywhere

he murmured as I led him away.

On the journey home he did not care

to talk, and my chief concern was to keep him wrapped in my greatcoat and to see that his bed was made ready as soon as I had restored him to his lodgings. The levatrice brought a quilted coverlet from her own room and hovered over him as gently as though he had been of the sex to require her services; while Agostino, at my summons, appeared with a bowl of hot soup that was heralded down the street by a reviving waft of garlic. To these ministrations I left the parocco, intending to call for news of him the next evening; but an unexpected pressure of work kept me late at my desk, and the following day some fresh obstacle delayed me.

On the third afternoon, as I was leaving the office, an agate-eyed infant from the Point hailed me with a message from the doctor. The parocco was worse and had asked for me. I jumped into the nearest car, and ten minutes later was running up the doctor's greasy stairs.

To my dismay I found Don Egidio's room cold and untenanted ; but I was reassured a moment later by the appearance of the levatrice, who announced that

she had transferred the blessed man to her own apartment, where he could have the sunlight and a good bed to lie in. There in fact he lay, weak but smiling, in a setting which contrasted oddly enough with his own monastic surroundings : a cheerful grimy room, hung with anecdotic chromos, photographs of lady - patients proudly presenting their offspring to the camera, and innumerable Neapolitan santolini decked out with shrivelled palm-leaves.

The levatrice whispered that the good man had the pleurisy, and that, as she phrased it, he was nearing his last milestone. I saw that he was in fact in a bad way, but his condition did not indicate any pressing danger, and I had the presentiment that he would still, as the saying is, put up a good fight. It was clear, however, that he knew what turn the conflict must take, and the solemnity with which he welcomed me showed that my summons was a part of that spiritual strategy with which the Catholic opposes the surprise of death.

" My son," he said, when the levatrice had left us, " I have a favour to ask you.

You found me yesterday bidding goodbye to my best friend." His cough interrupted him. " I have never told you," he went on, " the name of the family in which I was brought up. It was Siviano, and that was the grave of the Count's eldest son, with whom I grew up as a brother. For eighteen years he has lain in that strange ground— in terra aliena— and when I die, there will be no one to care for his grave."

I saw what he waited for. " I will care for it, signor parocco."

" I knew I should have your promise, my child; and what you promise you keep. But my friend is a stranger to you —you are young, and at your age life is a mistress who kisses away sad memories. Why should you remember the grave of a stranger ? I cannot lay such a claim on you. But I will tell you his story— and then I think that neither joy nor grief will let you forget him ; for when you rejoice you will remember how he sorrowed; and when you sorrow the thought of him will be like a friend's hand in yours,"

I

CRUCIAL INSTANCES

II

You tell me (Don Egidio began) that you know our little lake; and if you have seen it, you will understand why it always used to remind me of the "garden enclosed " of the Canticles.

Hortus inclusus; columba mea in foraminibus petrce; the words used to come back to me whenever I returned from a day's journey across the mountains, and looking down saw the blue lake far below, hidden in its hills like a happy secret in a stern heart. We were never envious of the glory of the great lakes. They are like the show pictures that some nobleman hangs in his public gallery; but our Iseo is the treasure that he hides in his inner chamber.

You tell me you saw it in summer, when it looks up like a saint's eye, reflecting the whole of heaven. It was then too that I first saw it. My future friend, the old Count, had found me at work on one of his fruit-farms up the valley, and hearing that I was ill-treated by my stepfather—a drunken pedlar from the Val

Mastellone, whom my poor mother a year or two earlier had come across at the fair of Lovere—he had taken me home with him to Iseo. I used to serve mass in our hill-village of Cerveno, and the village children called me "the little priest," because, when my work was done, I often crept back to the church to get away from my stepfather's blows and curses. " I will make a real priest of him," the Count declared; and that afternoon, perched on the box of his travelling-carriage, I was whirled away from the dark scenes of my childhood into a world where, as it seemed to me, every one was as happy as an angel on a presepio.

I wonder if you remember the Count's villa? It lies on the shore of the lake, facing the green knoll of Monte Isola, and overlooked by the village of Siviano and by the old parish church where I said mass for fifteen happy years. The village hangs on a ledge of the mountain; but the villa dips its foot in the lake, smiling at its reflection like a bather lingering on the brink. What Paradise it seemed to me that day! In our church up the valley there hung an old brown picture, with a

Saint Sebastian in the foreground; and behind him the most wonderful palace, with terraced gardens adorned with statues and fountains, where fine folk in resplendent dresses walked up and down without heeding the blessed martyr's pangs. The Count's villa, with its terraces, its roses, its marble steps descending to the lake, reminded me of that palace; only, instead of being inhabited by wicked people engrossed in their selfish pleasures, it was the home of the kindest friends that ever took a poor lad by the hand.

The old Count was a widower when I first knew him. He had been twice married, and his first wife had left him two children, a son and a daughter. The eldest, Donna Marianna, was then a girl of twenty, who kept her father's house and was a mother to the two lads. She was not handsome or learned, and had no taste for the world; but she was like the lavender-plant in a poor man's window—just a little grey flower, but a sweetness that fills the whole hoi. Her brother, Count Roberto, had been ailing from his birth, and was a studious lad with a melancholy, musing face such as you may see in some of Titian's portraits of young men. He looked like an exiled prince dressed in mourning. There was one child by the second marriage, Count Andrea, a boy of my own age, handsome as u Saint George, but not as kind as the others. No doubt, being younger, he was less able to understand why an uncouth peasant lad should have been brought to his father's table ; and the others were so fearful of hurting my feelings that, but for his teasing, I might never have mended my clumsy manners or learned how to behave in the presence of my betters. Count Andrea was not sparing in such lessons, and Count Roberto, in spite of his weak arms, chastised his brother roundly when he thought the discipline had been too severe; but, for my part, it seemed to me natural enough that such a god-like being should lord it over a poor clodhopper like my self.

Well, I will not linger over the beginning of my new life, for my story has to do with its close. Only I should like to make you understand what the change meant to me, an ignorant peasant lad, coming from hard words and blows and a smoke-blackened hut in the hills to that great house full of rare and beautiful things, and of beings who seemed to me even more rare and beautiful. Do you wonder I was ready to kiss the ground they trod, and would have given the last drop of my blood to serve them?

In due course I was sent to the seminary at Lodi; and on holidays I used to visit the family in Milan. Count Andrea was growing up to be one of the handsomest young men imaginable, but a trifle wild; and the old Count married him in haste to the daughter of a Venetian noble, who brought as her dower a great estate in Istria. The Countess Gemma, as this lady was called, was as light as thistledown, and had an eye like a baby's; but while she was cooing for the moon her pretty white hands were always stealing toward something within reach that she had not been meant to have. The old Count was not alert enough to follow these manoeuvres; and the Countess hid her designs under a torrent of guileless chatter, as pickpockets wear long sleeves to conceal their movements. Her only fault, he used to say, was that one of her aunts had married an Austrian; and this event having taken place before she was born, he laughingly acquitted her of any direct share in it. She confirmed his good opinion of her by giving her husband two sons; and Roberto showing no inclination to marry, these boys naturally came to be looked on as the heirs of the house.

Meanwhile, I had finished my course of studies, and the old Count, on my twenty-first birthday, had appointed me priest of the parish of Siviano. It was the year of Count Andrea's marriage, and there were great festivities at the villa. Three years later the old Count died, to the sorrow of his two eldest children. Donna Marianna and Count Roberto closed their apartments in the palace at Milan and withdrew for a year to Siviano. It was then that I first began to know my friend. Before that I had loved him without understanding him; now I learned of what metal he was made. His bookish tastes inclined him to a secluded way of living; and his younger brother perhaps -fancied that he would not care to assume the charge of the estate. But if Andrea thought this he was disappointed. Roberto resolutely took up the tradition of his father's rule, and, as if conscious of lacking the old Count's easy way with the peasants, made up for it by a redoubled zeal for their welfare. I have seen him toil for days to adjust some trifling difficulty that his father would have set right with a ready word; like the sainted bishop who, when a beggar asked him for a penny, cried out: "Alas, my brother, I have not a penny in my purse; but here are two gold pieces, if they can be made to serve you instead!" We had many conferences over the condition of his people, and he often sent me up the valley to look into the needs of the peasantry on the fruit-farms. No grievance was too trifling for him to consider it, no abuse too deep-seated for him to root it out; and many an hour that other men of his rank would have given to books or pleasure was devoted to adjusting a quarrel about boundary lines or to weighing the merits of a complaint against the tax collector. I often said that he was as much his people's priest as I; and he smiled and answered that every landowner was a king, and that in old days the king was always a priest.

Donna Marianna was urgent with him to marry, but he always declared that he had a family in his tenantry, and that, as for a wife, she had never let him feel the want of one. He had that musing temper which gives a man a name for coldness; though, in fact, he may all the while be storing fuel for a great conflagration. But to me he whispered another reason for not marrying. A man, he said, does not take wife and rejoice while his mother is on her death-bed ; and Italy, his mother, lay dying, with the foreign vultures waiting to tear her apart.

You are too young to know anything of those days, my son; and how can any one understand them who did not live through them ? Italy lay dying indeed ; but Lombardy was her heart, and her heart still beat, and sent the faint blood creeping to her cold extremities. Her torturers, weary of their work, had allowed her to fall into a painless stupor; but just as she was sinking from sleep to

death, Heaven sent Radetsky to scourge her back to consciousness; and at the first sting of his lash she sprang maimed and bleeding to her feet.

Ah, those days, those days, my son ! Italy—Italy—was the word on our lips ; but the thought in our hearts was just Austria. We clamoured for liberty, unity, the franchise; but under our breath we prayed only to smite the white-coats. Remove the beam from our eye, we cried, and we shall see our salvation clearly enough! We priests in the north were all liberals, and worked with the nobles and the men of letters. Gioberti was our breviary, and his Holiness, the new Pope, was soon to be the Tancred of our crusade. But meanwhile, mind you, all this went on in silence, underground as it were, while on the surface Lombardy still danced, feasted, married, and took office under the Austrian. In the iron mines up our valley there used to be certain miners who stayed below ground for months at a time; and, like one of these, Roberto remained buried in his purpose, while life went its way overhead. Though I was not in his confidence I knew well enough

where his thoughts were, for he went among us with the eye of a lover, the visionary look of one who hears a Voice. We all heard that Voice, to be sure, mingling faintly with the other noises of life; but to Roberto it was already as the roar of mighty waters, drowning every other sound with its thunder.

On the surface, as I have said, things looked smooth enough. An Austrian cardinal throned in Milan and an Austrian-hearted Pope ruled in Rome. In Lombardy, Austria couched like a beast of prey, ready to spring at our throats if we stirred or struggled. The Moderates, to whose party Count Roberto belonged, talked of prudence, compromise, the education of the masses; but if their words were a velvet sheath their thought was a dagger. For many years, as you know, the Milanese had maintained an outward show of friendliness with their rulers. The nobles had accepted office under the viceroy, and in the past there had been frequent intermarriage between the two aristocracies But now, one by one, the great houses had closed their doors against official

society. Though some of the younger and more careless, those who must dance and dine at any cost, still went to the palace and sat beside the enemy at the opera, fashion was gradually taking sides against them, and those who had once been laughed at as old fogeys were now applauded as patriots. Among these, of course, was Count Roberto, who for several years had refused to associate with the Austrians, and had silently resented his easy-going brother's disregard of political distinctions. Andrea and Gemma belonged to the moth tribe, who flock to the brightest light; and Gemma's Istrian possessions, and her family's connection with the Austrian nobility, gave them a pretext for fluttering about the viceregal candle. Roberto let them go their way, but his own course was a tacit protest against their conduct. They were always welcome at the Palazzo Siviano; but he and Donna Marianna withdrew from society in order to have an excuse for not showing themselves at the Countess Gemma's entertainments. If Andrea and Gemma were aware of his disapproval they were clever enough to ignore it ; for the rich elder brother who paid their debts and never meant to many was too important a person to be quarrelled with on political grounds. They seemed to think that if he married it would be only to spite them; and they were persuaded that their future depended on their giving him no cause to take such reprisals. I shall never be more than a plain peasant at heart, and I have little natural skill in discerning hidden motives, but the experience of the confessional gives every priest a certain insight into the secret springs of action, and I often wondered that the worldly wisdom of Andrea and Gemma did not help them to a clearer reading of their brother's character. For my part I knew that, in Roberto's heart, no great passion could spring from a mean motive; and I had always thought that if he ever loved any woman as he loved Italy, it must be from his country's hand that he received his bride. And so it came about.

Have you ever noticed, on one of those still autumn days before a storm, how here and there a yellow leaf will suddenly detach itself from the bough and whirl through the air as though some warning of the gale had reached it? So it was then in Lombardy. All round was the silence of decay; but now and then a word, a look, a trivial incident, fluttered ominously through the stillness. It was in '45. Only a year earlier the glorious death of the Bandiera brothers had sent a long shudder through Italy. In the Romagna, Renzi and his comrades had tried to uphold by action the protest set forth in the " Manifesto of Rimini" ; and their failure had sowed the seed which d'Azeglio and Cavour were to harvest. Everywhere the forces were silently gathering; and nowhere was the hush more profound, the least reverberation more audible, than in the streets of Milan.

It was Count Roberto's habit to attend early mass in the Cathedral; and one morning, as he was standing in the aisle, a young girl passed him with her father. Roberto knew the father, a beggarly Milanese of the noble family of Intelvi, who had cut himself off from his class by accepting an appointment in one of the Government offices. As the two went by he saw a group of Austrian officers looking after the girl, and heard one of them say : " Such a choice morsel as that is too good for slaves;" and another answer with a laugh: " Yes, it's a dish for the master's table!"

The girl heard too. She was as white as a wind-flower, and he saw the words come out on her cheek like a red mark from a blow. She whispered to her father, but he shook his head and drew her away without so much as a glance at the Austrians. Roberto heard mass, and then hastened out and placed himself in the porch of the Cathedral. A moment later the officers appeared, and they too stationed themselves near the doorway. Presently the girl came out on her father's arm. Her admirers stepped forward to greet Intelvi; and the cringing wretch stood there exchanging compliments with them, while their insolent stare devoured his daughter's beauty. She, poor thing, shook like a leaf, and her eyes, in avoiding theirs, suddenly encountered Roberto's. Her look was a wounded bird that flew to him for shelter. He carried it away in his breast and its live warmth beat against his heart. He thought that Italy had looked at him through those eyes; for love is the wiliest of masqueraders, and has a thousand disguises at his command.

Within a month Faustina Intelvi was his wife. Donna Marianna and I rejoiced ; for we knew he had chosen her because he loved her, and she seemed to us almost worthy of such a choice. As for Count Andrea and his wife, I leave you to guess what ingredients were mingled in the kiss with which they welcomed the bride. They were all smiles at Roberto's marriage, and had only words of praise for his wife. Donna Marianna, who had sometimes taxed me with suspecting their motives, rejoiced in this fresh proof of their magnanimity; but for my part I could have wished to see them a little less kind. All such twilight fears, however, vanished in the flush of my friend's happiness. Over some natures love steals gradually, as the morning light widens across a valley; but it had flashed on Roberto like the

leap of dawn to a snow-peak. He walked the world with the wondering step of a blind man suddenly restored to sight; and once he said to me with a laugh : " Love makes a Columbus of every one of us !"

And the Countess? The Countess, my son, was eighteen, and her husband was forty. Count Roberto had the heart of a poet, but he walked with a limp and his skin was sallow. Youth plucks the fruit for its colour rather than its flavour; and first love does not serenade its mistress on a church organ. In Italy girls are married as land is sold; if two estates adjoin two lives are united. As for the portionless girl, she is a knick-knack that goes to the highest bidder. Faustina was handed over to her purchaser as if she had been a picture for his gallery; and the transaction doubtless seemed as natural to her as to her parents. She walked to the altar like an Iphigenia; but pallour becomes a bride, and it looks well for a daughter to weep on leaving her mother. Perhaps it would have been different if she had guessed that the threshold of her new home was carpeted with love and its four

corners hung with tender thoughts of her; but her husband was a silent man, who never called attention to his treasures.

The great palace in Milan was a gloomy house for a girl to enter. Roberto and his sister lived in it as if it had been a monastery, going nowhere and receiving only those who laboured for the Cause. To Faustina, accustomed to the easy Austrian society, the Sunday evening receptions at the Palazzo Siviano must have seemed as dreary as a scientific congress. It pleased Roberto to regard her as a victim of barbarian insolence, an embodiment of his country desecrated by the desire of the enemy; but though, like any handsome penniless girl, Faustina had now and then been exposed to a free look or a familiar word, I doubt if she connected such incidents with the political condition of Italy. She knew, of course, that in marrying Siviano she was entering a house closed against the Austrian. One of Siviano's first cares had been to pension his father-in-law, with the stipulation that Intelvi should resign his appointment and give up all relations with the Government; and the old hypocrite, only too glad to

purchase idleness on such terms, embraced the liberal Cause with a zeal which left his daughter no excuse for half-heartedness. But he found it less easy than he had expected to recover a footing among his own people. In spite of his patriotic bluster the Milanese held aloof from him; and being the kind of man who must always take his glass in company, he gradually drifted back to his old associates. It was impossible to forbid Faustina to visit her parents; and in their house she breathed an air that was at least tolerant of Austria.

But I must not let you think that the young Countess appeared ungrateful or unhappy. She was silent and shy, and it needed a more enterprising temper than Roberto's to break down the barrier between them. They seemed to talk to one another through a convent-grating, rather than across a hearth ; but if Roberto had asked more of her than she could give, outwardly she was a model wife. She chose me at once as her confessor, and I watched over the first steps of her new life. Never was younger sister tenderer to her elder than she to Donna Marianna;

never was young wife more mindful of her religious duties, kinder to her dependents, more charitable to the poor; yet to be with her was like living in a room with shuttered windows. She was always the caged bird, the transplanted flower; for all Roberto's care she never bloomed or sang.

Donna Marianna was the first to speak of it. " The child needs more light and air," she said.

"Light? Air?" Roberto repeated. " Does she not go to mass every morning ? Does she not drive on the Corso every evening ?"

Donna Marianna was not called clever, but her heart was wiser than most women's heads.

"At our age, brother," said she, "the windows of the mind face north and look out on a landscape full of lengthening shadows. Faustina needs another outlook. She is as pale as a hyacinth grown in a cellar." Roberto himself turned pale, and I saw that she had uttered his own thought.

" You want me to let her go to Gemma's !" he exclaimed.

" Let her go wherever there is a little careless laughter."

" Laughter—now!" he cried, with a gesture toward the sombre line of portraits above his head.

"Let her laugh while she can, my brother."

That evening after dinner he called Faustina to him.

"My child," he said, "go and put on your jewels. Your sister Gemma gives a ball to-night, and the carriage waits to take you there. I am too much of a recluse to be at ease in such scenes, but I have sent word to your father to go with you."

Andrea and Gemma welcomed their young sister-in-law with effusion, and from that time she was often in their company. Gemma forbade any mention of politics in her drawing-room, and it was natural that Faustina should be glad to escape from the solemn conclaves of the Palazzo Siviano to a house where life went as gaily as in that villa above Florence where Boccaccio's careless storytellers took refuge from the plague. But meanwhile the political distemper was rapidly spreading, and in spite of Gemma's Austrian affiliations, it was no longer possible for her to receive the enemy openly. It was whispered that her door was still ajar to her old friends; but the rumour may have risen from the fact that one of the Austrian cavalry officers stationed at Milan was her own cousin, the son of the aunt on whose misalliance the old Count had so often bantered her. No one could blame the Countess Gemma for not turning her own flesh and blood out of doors; and the social famine to which the officers of the garrison were reduced made it natural that young Welkenstern should press the claims of consanguinity.

All this must have reached Roberto's ears ; but he made no sign, and his wife came and went as she pleased. When they returned the following year to the old dusky villa at Siviano she was like the voice of a brook in a twilight wood: one could not look at her without ransacking the spring for new similes to paint her freshness. With Roberto it was different. I found him older, more preoccupied and silent; but I guessed that his preoccupations were political, for when his eye rested on his wife it cleared like the lake when a cloud-shadow lifts from it.

Count Andrea and his wife occupied an adjoining villa ; and during k the villeg-giatura the two households lived almost as one family. Roberto, however, was often absent in Milan, called thither on business of which the nature was not hard to guess. Sometimes he brought back guests to the villa; and on these occasions Faustina and Donna Marianna went to Count Andrea's for the day. I have said that I was not in his confidence; but he knew my sympathies were with the liberals, and now and then he let fall a word of the work going on underground. Meanwhile the new Pope had been elected, and from Piedmont to Calabria we hailed in him the Banner that was to lead our hosts to war.

So time passed, and we reached the last months of '47. The villa on Iseo had been closed since the end of August. Roberto had no great liking for his gloomy palace in Milan, and it had been his habit to spend nine months of the year at Siviano; but he was now too much engrossed in his work to remain

away from Milan, and his wife and sister had joined him there as soon as the midsummer heat was over. During the autumn he had called me once or twice to the city to consult me on business connected with his fruit-farms; and in the course of our talks he had sometimes let fall a hint of graver matters. It was in July of that year that a troop of Croats had marched into Ferrara, with muskets and cannon loaded. The lighted matches of their cannon had fired the sleeping hate of Austria, and the whole country now echoed the Lombard cry: "Out with the barbarian!" All talk of ad-j ustment, compromise, reorganisation, shrivelled on lips that the live coal of patriotism had touched. Italy for the Italians, and then—monarchy, federation, republic, it mattered not what!

The oppressor's grip had tightened on our throats, and the clear-sighted saw well enough that Metternich's policy was to provoke a rebellion and then crush it under the Croat heel. But it was too late to cry prudence in Lombardy. With the first days of the new year the tobacco riots had drawn blood in Milan, Soon

afterward the Lion's Club was closed, and edicts were issued forbidding the singing of Pio Xono's hymn, the wearing of white and blue, the collecting of subscriptions for the victims of the riots. To each prohibition Milan returned a fresh defiance. The ladies of the nobility put on mourning for the rioters who had been shot down by the soldiery. Half the members of the Guardia Xobile resigned, and Count BoiTomeo sent back his Golden Fleece to the Emperor. Fresh regiments were continually pouring into Milan, and it was no secret that Radetsky was strengthening the fortifications. Late in January several leading liberals were arrested and sent into exile, and two weeks later martial law was proclaimed in Milan. At the first arrests several members of the liberal party had hastily left Milan, and I was not surprised to hear, a few days later, that orders had been given to reopen the villa at Siviano. The Count and Countess arrived there early in February.

It was seven months since I had seen the Countess, and I was struck with the change in her appearance. She was paler

than ever, and her step had lost its lightness. Yet she did not seem to share her husband's political anxieties; one would have said that she was hardly aware of them. She seemed wrapped in a veil of lassitude, like Iseo on a still grey morning, when dawn is blood-red on the mountains but a mist blurs its reflection in the lake. I felt as though her soul were slipping away from me, and longed to win her back to my care; but she made her ill-health a pretext for not coming to confession, and for the present I could only wait and carry the thought of her to the altar. She had not been long at Siviano before I discovered that this drooping mood was only one phase of her humour. Now and then she flung back the cowl of melancholy and laughed life in the eye; but next moment she was in shadow again, and her muffled thoughts had given us the slip. She was like the lake on one of those days when the wind blows twenty ways, and every promontory holds a gust in ambush.

Meanwhile there was a continual coming and going of messengers between Siviano and the city. They came mostly

at night, when the household slept, and were away again with the last shadows; but the news they brought stayed and widened, shining through every cranny of the old house. The whole of Lombardy was up. From Pavia to Mantua, from Como to Brescia, the streets ran blood like the arteries of one great body. At Pavia and Padua the universities were closed. The frightened viceroy was preparing to withdraw from Milan to Verona, and Radetsky continued to pour his men across the Alps, till a hundred thousand were massed between the Piave and the Ticino. And now every eye was turned to Turin. Ah, how we watched for the blue banner of Piedmont on the mountains! Charles Albert was pledged to our Cause; his whole people had armed to rescue us, the streets echoed with Avanti, Savoia/ and yet Savoy was silent and hung back. Each day was a lifetime strained to the cracking-point with hopes and disappointments. We reckoned the hours by rumours, the very minutes by hearsay. Then suddenly—ah, it was worth living through!—word came to us that Vienna was in revolt. The points

of the compass had shifted and our sun had risen in the north. I shall never forget that day at the villa. Roberto sent for me early, and I found him smiling and resolute, as becomes a soldier on the eve of action. He had made all his preparations to leave for Milan, and was awaiting a summons from his party. The whole household felt that great events impended, and Donna Marianna, awed and tearful, had pleaded with her brother that they should all receive the sacrament together the next morning. Roberto and his sister had been to confession the previous day, but the Countess Faustina had again excused herself. I did not see her while I was with the Count, but as I left the house she met me in the laurel walk. The morning was damp and cold, and she had drawn a black scarf over her hair, and walked with a listless dragging step; but at my approach she lifted her head quickly and signed to me to follow her into one of the recesses of clipped laurel that bordered the path.

"Don Egidio," she said, "you have heard the news?"

I assented.

"The Count goes to Milan to-morrow?"

"It seems probable, your Excellency."

"There will be fighting—we are on the eve of war, I mean?"

"We are in God's hands, your Excellency."

"In God's hands!" she murmured. Her eyes wandered and for a moment we stood silent; then she drew a purse from her pocket. "I was forgetting," she exclaimed. "This is for that poor girl you spoke to me about the other day— what was her name? The girl who met the Austrian soldier at the fair at Peschiera"

"Ah, Vannina," I said; "but she is dead, your Excellency."

"Dead!" She turned white, and the purse dropped from her hand. I picked it up and held it out to her, but she put back my hand. "That is for masses, then," she said; and with that she moved away toward the house.

I walked on to the gate; but before I had reached it I heard her step behind me.

"Don Egidio!" she called, and I turned back.

"You are coming to say mass in the chapel to-morrow morning?"

"That is the Count's wish."

She wavered a moment. "I am not well enough to walk up to the village this afternoon," she said at length. "Will you come back later and hear my confession here?"

"Willingly, your Excellency."

"Come at sunset, then." She looked at me gravely. "It is a long time since I have been to confession," she added.

"My child, the door of Heaven is always unlatched."

She made no answer, and I went my way.

I returned to the villa a little before sunset, hoping for a few words with Roberto. I felt with Faustina that we were on the eve of war, and the uncertainty of the outlook made me treasure every moment of my friend's company. I knew he had been busy all day, but hoped to find that his preparations were ended, and that he could spare me a half hour. I was not disappointed; for the servant who met me asked me to follow him to the Count's apartment. Roberto was sitting alone, with his back to the door, at a table spread with maps and papers. He stood up and turned an ashen face on me.

" Roberto ! " I cried, as if we had been boys together.

He signed to me to be seated.

" Egidio," he said suddenly, " my wife has sent for you to confess her ?"

"The Countess met me on my way home this morning and expressed a wish to receive the sacrament to-morrow morning with you and Donna Marianna, and I promised to return this afternoon to hear her confession."

Roberto sat silent, staring before him as though he hardly heard. At length he raised his head and began to speak.

" You have noticed lately that my wife has been ailing ?" he asked.

"Every one must have seen that the Countess is not in her usual health. She has seemed nervous, out of spirits— I have fancied that she might be anxious about your Excellency."

He leaned across the table and laid his wasted hand on mine. " Call me Roberto," he said.

There was another pause before he went on. " Since I saw you this morning/' he said slowly, " something horrible has happened. After you left I sent for Andrea and Gemma to tell them the news from Vienna, and the probability of my being summoned to Milan before night. You know as well as I that we have reached a crisis. There will be fighting within twenty-four hours, if I know my people; and war may follow sooner than we think. I felt it my duty to leave my affairs in Andrea's hands, and to entrust my wife to his care. Don't look startled," he added with a faint smile, "no reasonable man goes on a journey without setting his house in order; and if things take the turn I expect, it may be some months before you see me back at Siviano.—But it was not to hear this that I sent for you." He pushed his chair aside and walked up and down the room with his short limping step. " My God !" he broke out wildly, " how can I say it ?—When Andrea had heard me, I saw him exchange a glance with his wife, and she said with that infernal sweet voice of hers, 'Yes, Andrea, it is our duty. 1

" Your duty?' I asked. ' What is your duty ? '

" Andrea wetted his lips with his tongue and looked at her again; and her look was like a blade in his hand.

" Your wife has a lover,' he said.

"She caught my arm as I flung myself on him. He is ten times stronger than I, but you remember how I made him howl for mercy in the old days when he used to bully you.

"' Let me go,' I said to his wife. ' He must live to unsay it.'

" Andrea began to whimper. * Oh, my poor brother, I would give my heart's blood to unsay it! '

"'The secret has been killing us,' she chimed in.

"'The secret? Whose secret? How dare you?'

"Gemma fell on her knees like a tragedy actress. ' Strike me— kill me—it is I who am the offender! It was at my house that she met him '

"'Him?'

" ' Franz Welkenstern—my cousin,' she wailed.

" I suppose I stood before them like a stunned ox, for they repeated the name again and again, as if they were not sure of my having heard it.—Not hear it I " he cried suddenly, dropping into a chair and hiding his face in his hands. " Shall I ever on earth hear anything else again ?"

He sat a long time with his face hidden, and I waited. My head was like a great bronze bell with one thought for the clapper.

After a while he went on in a low, deliberate voice, as though his words were balancing themselves on the brink of madness. With strange composure he repeated each detail of his brother's charges: the meeting in the Countess Gemma's drawing-room, the innocent friendliness of the two young people, the talk of mysterious visits to a villa outside the Porta Ticinese, the ever-widening circle of scandal that had spread about their names. At first, Andrea said, he and his wife had refused to listen to the reports which reached them. Then, when the talk became too loud, they had sent for Welkenstern,

remonstrated with him, implored him to exchange into another regiment, but in vain. The young officer indignantly denied the reports, and declared that to leave his post at such a moment would be desertion.

With a laborious accuracy, Roberto went on, detailing one by one each incident of the hateful story, till suddenly he cried out, springing from his chair— "And now to leave her with this lie unburied! "

His cry was like the lifting of a gravestone from my breast. "You must not leave her!" I exclaimed.

He shook his head. " I am pledged."

" This is your first duty."

" It would be any other man's ; not an Italian's."

I was silent: in those days the argument seemed unanswerable.

At length I said : " No harm can come to her while you are away. Donna Marianna and I are here to watch over her. And when you come back "

He looked at me gravely. " I come back-

" Roberto!"

CRUCIAL INSTANCES

" We are men, Egidio; we both know what is coming. Milan is up already; and there is a rumour that Charles Albert is moving. This year the spring rains will be red in Italy."

" In your absence not a breath shall touch her!"

" And if I never come back to defend her ? They hate her as hell hates, Egidio ! —They kept repeating, ' He is of her own

age, and youth draws youth She is

in their way, Egidio ! "

" Consider, my son. They do not love her, perhaps; but why should they hate her at such cost ? She has given you no child."

" No child 1" He paused. " But what

if ? She has ailed lately !" he cried,

and broke off to grapple with the stabbing thought.

" Roberto ! Roberto !" I adjured him.

He jumped up and gripped my arm.

" Egidio ! You believe in her ?"

" She's as pure as a lily on the altar !"

" Those eyes are wells of truth—and she has been like a daughter to Marianna.— Egidio ! do I look like an old man ?"

" Quiet yourself, Roberto," I entreated,

" Quiet myself? With this sting in my blood ? A lover—and an Austrian lover! Oh, Italy, Italy, my bride !"

" I stake my life on her truth," I cried, " and who knows better than I ? Has her soul not lain before me like the bed of a clear stream ?"

"And if what you saw there was only the reflection of your faith in her?"

" My son, I am a priest, and the priest penetrates to the soul as the angel passed through the walls of Peter's prison. I see the truth in her heart as I see Christ in the host!"

" No, no, she is false!" he cried.

I sprang up terrified. " Roberto, be silent!"

He looked at me with a wild incredulous smile. " Poor simple man of God !" he said.

" I would not exchange my simplicity for yours — the dupe of envy's first malicious whisper!"

« Envy—you think that ?"

" Is it questionable ?"

" You would stake your life on it ?"

"My life!"

" Your faith ? "

" My faith!"

" Your vows as a priest ?"

" My vows " I stopped and stared at

him. He had risen and laid his hand on my shoulder.

"You see now what I would be at," he said quietly. " I must take your place presently "

"My place— -?"

"When my wife comes down. You understand me."

" Ah, now you are quite mad !" I cried, breaking away from him.

" Am I ?" he returned, maintaining his strange composure."Consider a moment. She has not confessed to you before since our return from Milan "

" Her ill-health-

He cut me short with a gesture. " Yet to-day she sends for you "

"In order that she may receive the sacrament with you on the eve of your first separation."

" If that is her only reason, her first words will clear her. I must hear those words, Egidio!"

" You are quite mad," I repeated,

" Strange," he said slowly. " You stake your life on my wife's innocence, yet you refuse me the only means of vindicating it!"

" I would give my life for any one of you—but what you ask is not mine to give."

" The priest first—the man afterward ?" he sneered.

" Long afterward !"

He measured me with a contemptuous eye. " We laymen are ready to give the last shred

of flesh from our bones, but you priests intend to keep your cassocks whole."

"I tell you my cassock is not mine," I repeated.

"And, by God," he cried, "you are right; for it's mine! Who put it on your back but my father? What kept it there but my charity? Peasant! beggar! Hear his holiness pontificate!"

"Yes," I said, "I was a peasant and a beggar when your father found me; and if he had left me one I might have been excused for putting my hand to any ugly job that my betters required of me; but he made me a priest, and so set me above all of you, and laid on me the charge of your souls as well as mine."

He sat down shaken with dreadful tears. "Ah," he broke out, "would you have answered me thus when we were boys together, and I stood between you and Andrea?"

"If God had given me the strength."

"You call it strength to make a woman's soul your stepping-stone to heaven?"

"Her soul is in my care, not yours, my son. She is safe with me."

"She? But I? I go out to meet death, and leave a worse death behind me!" He leaned over and clutched my arm. "It is not for myself I plead, but for her—for her, Egidio! Don't you see to what a hell you condemn her if I don't come back? What chance has she against that slow unsleeping hate? Their lies will fasten themselves to her and suck out her life. You and Marianna are powerless against such enemies."

"You leave her in God's hands, my son."

"Easily said—but, ah, priest, if you were a man! What if their poison works in me and I go to battle thinking that every Austrian bullet may be sent by her lover's hand? What if I die not only to free Italy but to free my wife as well?"

I laid my hand on his shoulder. "My son, I answer for her. Leave your faith in her in my hands and I will keep it whole."

He stared at me strangely. "And what if your own fail you?"

"In her? Never. I call every saint to witness!"

"And yet—and yet—ah, this is a blind," he shouted; "you know all and perjure yourself to spare me!"

At that, my son, I felt a knife in my breast. I looked at him in anguish, and his gaze was a wall of metal. Mine seemed to slip away from it, like a claw-less thing struggling up the sheer side of a precipice.

"You know all,' 1 he repeated, "and you dare not let me hear her!"

"I dare not betray my trust."

He waved the answer aside.

"Is this a time to quibble over church discipline? If you believed in her, you would save her at any cost!"

I said to myself: "Eternity can hold nothing worse than this for me"
and clutched my resolve again like a cross to my bosom.

Just then there was a hand on the door, and we heard Donna Marianna.

"Faustina has sent to know if the signor parocco is here."

"He is here. Bid her come down to the chapel." Roberto spoke quietly, and closed the door on her so that she should not see his face. We heard her patter away across the brick floor of the salone.

Roberto turned to me. " Egidio !" he said; and all at once I was no more than a straw on the torrent of his will.

The chapel adjoined the room in which we sat. He opened the door, and in the twilight I saw the light glimmering before the Virgin's shrine and the old carved confessional standing like a cowled watcher in its corner. But I saw it all in a dream; for nothing in heaven or earth was real to me but the iron grip on my shoulder.

" Quick!" he said, and drove me forward. I heard him shoot back the bolt of the outer door, and a moment

later I stood alone in the garden. The sun had set and the cold spring dusk was falling. Lights shone here and there in the long front of the villa; the statues glimmered grey among the thickets. Through the window-pane of the chapel I caught the faint red gleam of the Virgin's lamp; but I turned my back on it and walked away.

All night 1 lay like a heretic on the fire. Before dawn there came a call from the villa. The Count had received a second summons from Milan and was to set out in an hour. I hurried down the cold dewy path to the lake. All was new and hushed and strange, as on the day of resurrection; and in the dark twilight of the garden alleys the statues stared at me like the shrouded dead.

In the salone, where the old Count's portrait hung, I found the family assembled. Andrea and Gemma sat together, a little pinched, I thought, but decent and self-contained, like mourners who expect to inherit. Donna Marianna drooped near them, with something black over her head, and her face dim with weeping. Roberto received me calmly, and then turned to his sister.

" Go, fetch my wife," he said.

While she was gone there was silence. We could hear the cold drip of the garden-fountain and the patter of rats in the wall. Andrea and his wife stared out of the window and Roberto sat in his father's carved seat at the head of the long table. Then the door opened and Faustina entered.

When I saw her I stopped breathing. She seemed no more than the shell of herself, a hollow thing that grief has voided. Her eyes returned our images like polished agate, but conveyed to her no sense of our presence. Marianna led her to a seat, and she crossed her hands and nailed her dull gaze on Roberto. I looked from one to another, and in that spectral light it seemed to me that we were all souls come to judgment, and naked to each other as to God. As to my own wrong-doing, it weighed on me no more than dust. The only feeling I had room for was fear— a fear that seemed to fill my throat and lungs, and bubble coldly over my drowning head.

Suddenly Roberto began to speak. His voice was clear and steady, and I clutched at his words to drag myself above the surface of my terror. He touched on the charge that had been made against his wife—he did not say by whom—the foul rumour that had made itself heard on the eve of their first parting. Duty, he said, had sent him a double summons; to fight for his country and for his wife. He must clear his wife's name before he was worthy to draw sword for Italy. There was no time to tame the slander before throttling it; he had to take the shortest way to its throat. At this point he looked at me and my soul shook. Then he turned to Andrea and Gemma.

" When you came to me with this rumour," he said quietly, "you agreed to consider the family honour satisfied if I could induce Don Egidio to let me take his place and overhear my wife's confession, and if that confession convinced me of her innocence. Was this the understanding ?"

Andrea muttered something and Gemma tapped a sullen foot.

CEUCIAL INSTANCES

" After you had left," Roberto continued, " I laid the case before Don Egidio and threw myself on his mercy." He looked at me fixedly. " So strong was his faith in my wife's innocence that for her sake he agreed to violate the sanctity of the confessional. I took his place."

Marianna sobbed and crossed herself, and a strange look flitted over Faustina's face.

There was a moment's pause; then Roberto, rising, walked across the room to his wife and took her by the hand.

"Your seat is beside me, Countess Siviano," he said, and led her to the empty chair by his own.

Gemma started to her feet, but her husband pulled her down again.

" Jesus ! Mary !" we heard Donna Marianna moan.

Roberto raised his wife's hand to his lips. "You forgive me," he said, "the means I took to defend you ?" And turning to Andrea he added slowly : " I declare my wife innocent, and my honour satisfied. You swear to stand by my decision ?"

What Andrea stammered out, what hissing serpents of speech Gemma's clinched teeth bit back, I never knew— for my eyes were on Faustina, and her face was a wonder to behold.

She had let herself be led across the room like a blind woman, and had listened without change of feature to her husband's first words ; but as he ceased her frozen gaze broke and her whole body seemed to melt against his breast. He put his arm out, but she slipped to his feet and Marianna hastened forward to raise her up. At that moment we heard the stroke of oars across the quiet water and saw the Count's boat touch the landing-steps. Four strong oarsmen from Monte I sola were to row him down to Iseo, to take horse for Milan, and his servant, knapsack on shoulder, knocked warningly at the terrace window.

"No time to lose, Excellency!" he cried.

Roberto turned and gripped my hand. " Pray for me," he said low; and with a brief gesture to the others ran down the terrace to the boat.

Marianna was bathing Faustina with happy tears.

"Look up, dear! Think how soon he will come back! And there is the sunrise—see !"

Andrea and Gemma had slunk away like ghosts at cock-crow, and a red dawn stood over Milan.

If that sun rose red it set scarlet. It was the first of the Five Days in Milan —the Five Glorious Days, as they are called. Roberto reached the city just before the gates closed. So much we knew—little more. We heard of him in the Broletto (whence he must have escaped when the Austrians blew in the door) and in the Casa Vidiserti, with Casati, Cattaneo, and the rest; but after the barricading began we could trace him only as having been seen here and there in the thick of the fighting, or tending the wounded under Bertani's orders. His place, one would have said, was in the council-chamber, with the soberer heads; but that was an hour when every man gave his blood where it was most needed, and Cernuschi, Dandolo, Anfossi, della Porta fought shoulder to shoulder with students, artisans and peasants. Certain it is that he was seen on the fifth day; for among the volunteers who swarmed after Manara in his assault on the Porta Tosa was a servant of the Palazzo Siviano; and this fellow swore he had seen his master charge with Manara in the last assault—had watched him, sword in hand, press close to the gates, and then, as they swung open before the victorious dash of our men, had seen him drop and disappear in the inrushing tide of peasants that almost swept the little company off its feet. After that we heard nothing. There was savage work in Milan in those days, and more than one well-known figure lay lost among the heaps of dead, hacked and disfeatured by Croat blades.

At the villa we waited breathless. News came to us hour by hour; the very wind seemed to carry it, and it was swept to us on the incessant rush of the rain. On the twenty-third Radetsky had fled from Milan, to face Venice rising in his path. On the twenty-fourth the first Piedmontese had crossed the Ticino, and Charles Albert himself was in Pavia on the twenty-ninth. The bells of Milan had carried the word from Turin to Naples, from Genoa to Ancona, and the whole country was pouring like a flood-tide into Lombardy. Heroes sprang up from the bloody soil as thick as wheat after rain, and every day carried some new name to us, but never the one for which we prayed and waited. Weeks passed. We heard of Pastrengo, Goito, Rivoli; of Radetsky hemmed into the Quadrilateral, and our troops closing in on him from Rome, Tuscany and Venetia. Months passed—and we heard of Custozza. We saw Charles Albert's broken forces flung back from the Mincio to the Oglio, from the Oglio to the Adda. We followed the dreadful retreat from Milan, and saw our rescuers dispersed like dust before the wind. But all the while no word came to us of Roberto.

These were dark days in Lombardy; and nowhere darker than in the old villa on Iseo. In September Donna Marianna and the young Countess put on black, and Count Andrea and his wife followed their example. In October the Countess gave birth to a daughter. Count Andrea then took possession of the Palazzo Siviano, and the two women remained at the villa. I have no heart to tell you of the days that followed. Donna Marianna wept and prayed incessantly, and it was long before the baby could snatch a smile from her. As for the Countess Faustina, she went among us like one of the statues in the garden. The child had a wet-nurse from the village, and it was small wonder there was no milk for it in that marble breast. I spent much of my time at the villa, comforting Donna Marianna as best I could; but sometimes, in the long winter evenings, when we three sat in the dimly-lit salone, with the old Count's portrait overhead, and I looked up and saw the Countess Faustina in the tall carved seat beside her husband's empty chair, my spine grew chill and I felt a cold wind in my hair.

The end of it was that in the spring I went to see my bishop and laid my sin before him. He was a saintly and merciful old man, and gave me a patient hearing.

"You believed the lady innocent?" he asked when I had ended.

" Monsignore, on my soul!"

" You thought to avert a great calamity from the house to which you owed more than your life ?"

" It was my only thought."

He laid his hand on my shoulder.

" Go home, my son. You shall learn my decision."

Three months later I was ordered to resign my living and go to America, where a priest was needed for the Italian mission church in New York. I packed my possessions and set sail from Genoa. I knew no more of America than any peasant up in the hills. I fully expected to be speared by naked savages on landing; and for the first few months after my arrival I wished at least once a day that such a blessed fate had befallen me. But it is no part of my story to tell you what I suffered in those early days. The Church had dealt with me mercifully, as is her wont, and her punishment fell far below my deserts. . .

I had been some four years in New

York, and no longer thought of looking back from the plough, when one day word was brought me that an Italian professor lay ill and had asked for a priest. There were many Italian refugees in New York at that time, and the greater number, being well-educated men, earned a living by teaching their language, which was then included among the accomplishments of fashionable New York. The messenger led me to a poor boarding-house and up to a small bare room on the top floor. On the visiting-card nailed to the door I read the name " De Roberti, Professor of Italian." Inside, a grey-haired haggard man tossed on the narrow bed. He turned a glazed eye on me as I entered, and I recognised Roberto Siviano.

I steadied myself against the door-post, and stood staring at him without a word.

" What's the matter ?" asked the doctor who was bending over the bed. I stammered that the sick man was an old friend.

"He wouldn't know his oldest friend just now," said the doctor. " The fever's on him; but it will go down toward sunset."

I sat down at the head of the bed and took Roberto's hand in mine.

"Is he going to die?" I asked.

"I don't believe so; but he wants nursing."

" I will nurse him."

The doctor nodded and went out. I sat in the little room, with Roberto's burning hand in mine. Gradually his skin cooled, the ringers grew quiet, and the flush faded from his sallow cheekbones. Towards dusk he looked up at me and smiled.

" Egidio," he said quietly.

I administered the sacrament, which he received with the most fervent devotion; then he fell into a deep sleep.

During the weeks that followed I had no time to ask myself the meaning of it all. My one business was to keep him alive if I could. I fought the fever day and night, and at length it yielded. For the most part he raved or lay unconscious, but now and then he knew me for a moment, and whispered " Egidio," with a look of peace.

I had stolen many hours from my duties to nurse him; and as soon as the danger was past I had to go back to my parish work. Then it was that I began to ask myself what had brought him to America, but I dared not face the answer.

On the fourth day I snatched a moment from my work and climbed to his room. I found him sitting propped against his pillows, weak as a child, but clear-eyed and quiet. I ran forward, but his look stopped me.

" Signor parocco" he said, " the doctor tells me that I owe my life to your nursing, and I have to thank you for the kindness you have shown to a friendless stranger."

" A stranger ? " I gasped.

He looked at me steadily. " I am not aware that we have met before," he said.

For a moment I thought the fever was on him, but a second glance convinced me that he was master of himself.

" Roberto ! " I cried, trembling.

" You have the advantage of me," he said civilly. " But my name is Roberti, not Roberto."

The floor swam under me and I had to lean against the wall.

"You are not Count Roberto Siviano of Milan?"

"I am Tommaso de Roberti, Professor of Italian, from Modena."

"And you have never seen me before?"

"Never that I know of."

"Were you never at Siviano, on the lake of Iseo?" I faltered.

He said calmly: "I am unacquainted with that part of Italy."

My heart grew cold and I was silent.

"You mistook me for a friend, I suppose?" he added.

"Yes," I cried, "I mistook you for a friend;" and with that I fell on my knees by his bed and cried like a child.

Suddenly I felt a touch on my shoulder. "Egidio," said he in a broken voice, "look up."

I raised my eyes, and there was his old smile above me, and we clung to each other without a word. Presently, however, he drew back, and put me quietly aside.

"Sit over there, Egidio. My bones are like water and I am not good for much talking yet."

"Let us wait, Roberto. Sleep now— we can talk to-morrow."

"No. What I have to say must be said at once." He examined me thoughtfully. "You have a parish here in New York?"

I assented.

"And my work keeps me here. I have pupils. It is too late to make a change."

"A change?"

He continued to look at me calmly. "It would be difficult for me," he explained, "to find employment in a new place."

"But why should you leave here?"

"I shall have to," he returned deliberately, "if you persist in recognising in me your former friend, Count Siviano."

"Roberto!"

He lifted his hand. "Egidio," he said, "I am alone here, and without friends. The companionship, the sympathy of my parish priest would be a consolation in this strange city; but it must not be the companionship of the parocco of Siviano. You understand?"

"Roberto," I cried, "it is too dreadful to understand!"

"Be a man, Egidio," said he, with a touch of impatience. "The choice lies with you, and you must make it now. If you are willing to ask no questions, to name no names, to make no allusions to the past, let us live as friends together, in God's name! If not, as soon as my legs can carry me, I must be off again. The world is wide luckily—but why should we be parted?"

I was on my knees at his side in an instant. "We must never be parted!" I cried. "Do as you will with me. Give me your orders and I obey—have I not always obeyed you?"

I felt his hand close sharply on mine. "Egidio!" he admonished me.

"No—no—I shall remember. I shall say nothing"

"Think nothing?"

"Think nothing," I said with a last effort.

"God bless you!" he answered.

My son, for eight years I kept my word to him. We met daily almost, we ate and walked and talked together, we lived like David and Jonathan—but without so much as a glance at the past. How he had escaped from Milan—how he had reached New York — I never knew. We talked often of Italy's liberation —as what Italians would not ? — but never touched on his share in the work. Once only a word slipped from him ; and that was when one day he asked me how it was that I had been sent to America. The blood rushed to my face, and before I could answer he had raised a silencing hand.

" I see," he said ; "it was your penance too."

During the first years he had plenty of work to do, but he lived so frugally that I guessed he had some secret use for his earnings. It was easy to conjecture what it was. All over the world Italian exiles were toiling and saving to further the great Cause. He had political friends in New York, and sometimes he went to other cities to attend meetings and make addresses. His zeal never slackened ; and but for me he would often have gone hungry that some shivering patriot might dine. I was with him heart and soul, but I had the parish on my shoulders, and perhaps my long experience of men had made me a little less credulous than u

Christian charity requires; for I could have sworn that some of the heroes who hung on him had never had a whiff of Austrian blood, and would have fed out of the same trough with the white-coats if there had been polenta enough to go round. Happily, my friend had no such doubts. He believed in the patriots as devoutly as in the Cause; and if some of his hard-earned dollars travelled no farther than the nearest wine-cellar or cigar-shop, he never suspected the course they took.

His health was never the same after the fever; and by and by he began to lose his pupils, and the patriots cooled off as his pockets fell in. Toward the end I took him to live in my shabby attic. He had grown weak and had a troublesome cough, and he spent the greater part of his days indoors. Cruel days they must have been to him, but he made no sign, and always welcomed me with a cheerful word. When his pupils dropped off, and his health made it difficult for him to pick up work outside, he set up a letter-writer's sign, and used to earn a few pennies by serving as amanuensis to my poor parishioners; but it went against him to take their money, and half the time he did the work for nothing. I knew it was hard for him to live on charity, as he called it, and I used to find what jobs I could for him among my friends, the negozianti, who would send him letters to copy, accounts to make up and what not; but we were all poor together, and the master had licked the platter before the dog got it.

So lived that just man, my son ; and so, after eight years of exile, he died one day in my arms. God had let him live long enough to see Solferino and Villafranca; and was perhaps never more merciful than in sparing him Monte Rotondo and Mentana. But these are things of which it does not become me to speak. The new Italy does not wear the face of our visions; but it is written that God shall know His own, and it cannot be that He shall misread the hearts of those who dreamed of fashioning her in His image.

As for my friend, he is at peace, I doubt not; and his just life and holy death intercede for me, who sinned for his sake alone.

THE END

Printed in Great Britain
by Amazon